STONES

for my

FATHER

TRILBY KENT

TUNDRA BOOKS

Published in Canada by Tundra Books,
75 Sherbourne Street, Toronto, Ontario M5A 2P9

Published in the United States by Tundra Books of Northern New York,
P.O. Box 1030, Plattsburgh, New York 12901

Library of Congress Control Number: 2010928790

Library and Archives Canada Cataloguing in Publication
Kent, Trilby
Medina Hill / Trilby Kent.

ISBN 978-1-77049-252-3

I. Title.

PS8571.E643S76 2011   jC813'.54   C2010-903163-6

We acknowledge the financial support of the Government of Canada
through the Book Publishing Industry Development Program (BPIDP) and
that of the Government of Ontario through the Ontario Media
Development Corporation's Ontario Book Initiative. We further acknowledge the support of the Canada Council for the Arts and the Ontario Arts
Council for our publishing program.

Typset in Garamond by Tundra, Toronto
Printed and bound in Canada

This book is printed on acid-free paper that is 100% recycled,
ancient-forest friendly (100% post-consumer recycled).

1   2   3   4   5   6   16   15   14   13   12   11

In memory of those who came before me —
the sons and daughters of the prairie and veld.

ALSO BY TRILBY KENT

Medina Hill

CONTENTS

NTOMBAZI

My mother once told me of a dream she had as a young girl, in the days before the English came. She had dreamed of a child, a boy, with ruddy cheeks and blue eyes like my father's, and a gurgling laugh that could make even Oom Jakob smile.

I was not that child. My mother would have to wait four long years before another baby came along, not counting the one that was stillborn shortly after my third birthday. Eleven months later, Gert arrived: a squalling, sticky, red-faced putto whose body was all out of proportion and who smelled like parsnips and brine. When my mother laid eyes on him for the first time, the look on her face told me that this, *this* was the child of her dream.

"You see, Corlie – eyes just like his father's," she said, while Tant Minna fussed about the bed with clean towels and a basin of hot water. "And so much hair, *boytjie!*"

There were many things that set Gert and me apart, but — as far as I could tell — those were the important ones. Gertie's hair grew into golden curls, while mine remained coarse and tawny. Gertie's eyes were the color of veld violets, while mine were like pools of muddy water. When Hansie was born a few years later, he was the same: blond and bouncing, with cornflower eyes and my Oupa Wessel's jug ears. No one ever thought to comment on my looks. My arms were too skinny and my front teeth overlapped slightly. The skin on my nose turned pink and peeled after just a few minutes in the African sun.

"My little *rooineus*," Pa used to say when, as a young girl, I would clamber into his lap and lock my arms around his shoulders. *Rooinek* was the word we used for the English — "rednecks," because they burned so easily in the sun — but my father's name for me was always used with a smile and a wink.

My mother never called me anything but Corlie. If she used my full name, Coraline Roux, I knew that it was time to make myself scarce by hiding in the cattle sheds.

She'd used my full name the morning I dropped a jar of peaches in the kitchen. The impact sent juice splashing across the slate tiles and a million shards of glass cartwheeling about the floor. When my mother bent to salvage some of the preserved fruit, she must have cut a finger with a piece of glass because immediately she shot upright with a gasped "*Godverdomme!*" and cuffed me sharply about the ear.

"Get out of here," she snapped. "Take your brother to Oom Flip's. He owes us a box of tobacco." Despite her godly airs, my mother was a prodigious smoker. Pa had never approved of her pipe habit, but Pa wasn't around anymore to tell her so. My mother's face had turned quite red, the veins in her temples bulging where her hair had been scraped back into a severe bun. "Are you deaf, girl? Do you want me to get the *sjambok?*"

The whip was made of rhino hide and had only ever been used by my father for cattle driving. I didn't wait for a second threat but scarpered right then and there, grabbing Gert's hand as I passed him on the stoop and hauling him behind me until we were safely out of view from the house.

Oom Flip wasn't really our uncle. He owned the trading shop halfway between our farm and Amersfoort, about an hour's walk under a high sun. Oom Flip se Winkel sold everything that we couldn't grow or raise or make ourselves, such as tobacco. The shop smelled of leather and dried fish, and the sour beer that local men brewed from sorghum. Sometimes, when his wife wasn't around, Oom Flip would pass us a couple of syrupy twisted doughnuts as a treat.

Beyond the dirt track that led to Amersfoort, a gray-green plateau scattered with aloes stretched all the way to the Drakensberg Mountains. The jacaranda tree next to our clay-brick house was the tallest thing for miles. From where we paused atop a *koppie,* the white farm buildings behind us seemed to huddle close to the dry land as if to escape the sun's searching glare. On one side of the hill were fields of hardy, fragrant lavender plants buzzing with bees drunk on wild nectar; on the other, clusters of crackled spurge shrubs and an expanse of yellow grassland. In the distance, a shepherd herded a few goats across the rugged terrain. The smell of hot, sweet grass filled the air.

"What if there are khakis?" asked Gert as he stumbled along beside me. "What if they see us?"

"Don't be stupid," I said. "There aren't any English here – they learned their lesson at Bergendal. The Transvaal is free Boer country now."

My little brother scowled down at his feet. There'd not been time to collect our shoes from the house, and his toenails were black with grit. When the heat grew so fierce that even the crickets seemed to droop during their music-making, I would often discard my pinafore and stockings and make do in the grubby shift that had grown stiff with Ma's zealous scrubbing. For the boys, it was easier: Gert seemed to live in the same pair of breeches, with just a single suspender to preserve his modesty. Even Ma agreed that in these hard times it was only sensible to keep our better clothes intact for winter.

After we had been walking for several minutes, my brother pointed at a herd of springbok edging along the horizon.

"We should be hunting," he murmured. "If Pa were here, we'd be eating eland and blesbok every night."

"Shut up," I said. Gert knew full well that there was no point in talking as if Pa was coming back. There was no coming back from where Pa had gone.

"I'm hungry."

"We'll ask Tant Sanna for some mealie bread at the shop."

We kept walking.

"Tell me a story, Corlie."

It was a request that he knew I wouldn't be able to resist. Ma always said that my stories would only get me into trouble, that a good Boer girl should spend more time learning how to skin game and mend her brothers' pants – and less time spinning lies for their amusement. "Twelve years old and still wasting your breath on fairy tales," she would say. "It's high time you turned your mind to the Bible, my girl. There are plenty of stories in the Good Book – and all of them true, not just the silly ideas of an idle *domkop*."

But the Bible didn't have stories about the *tokoloshe* that lived under my bed, a mischievous spirit that could make itself invisible by swallowing a stone. The Bible didn't have stories about men who survived in the desert by gutting an oryx and drinking the contents of its stomach. The Bible didn't even have the best story of all – which Pa had told me himself as soon as I was old enough to understand – about how the Boers trekked for many years through wild and dangerous bush before settling in the Transvaal. "Africa defeats some people and redeems others," Pa used to tell me. "The *Boere* can't be defeated by Africa, because it is ours. God gave it to us."

But Gert had heard these stories before, so I decided to tell him a new one. It was a tale that I had been working on for several days, about a queen who wore a luminous boa constrictor as a cowl and a little green gecko as a brooch. Ostrich feathers decorated her hair, a necklace of cowrie shells circled her neck, and her dress was made of red-bush leaves and zebra skins. I called her Ntombazi, after the Zulu queen.

I was halfway into the story when my brother let out a howl of pain, crumpling to the ground and grabbing his left foot with both hands.

"What is it, Gertie?" I dropped to my knees and pried open my brother's clasped fingers, already imagining the worst: a scorpion bite, perhaps, or a snake . . .

"An arrowhead!" My brother's round face lit up; he hadn't even noticed the crimson blood rising in a bubble from his big toe. He turned the flint point this way and that, studying its carved edges against the sky. "Bushman. I wonder how old it is . . ."

I ripped an aloe leaf from a nearby plant and pressed it against the wound. "Is that better? Can you walk? Shall I help you?"

Gert shot me a scornful look. "*Ag, no!*" he said, pushing me away with his other heel. My brother was only eight, and already he was learning to talk like a big man. "I'm not a baby, Corlie." He stood up, all the while examining his precious trophy. "I'll bore a hole through it and wear it around my neck," he said, more to himself than to me.

At Oom Flip's, the shopkeeper's wife gave us some fudge to suck on while she cleaned Gert's wound with rubbing alcohol. Tant Sanna was a buxom old auntie with the haunches of a warhorse and whiskers as thick as sewing needles sprouting from her chin. My brother squirmed a bit, but he was too proud to cry the way he might have if it had been Ma tending to him. When Oom Flip came in, bearing two magnificent pumpkins from their garden, he grinned at the sight of us.

"Been in the wars, eh, Gert?" he asked, his voice rumbling like distant thunder as he set the pumpkins on the counter by the till. "Let's see to that."

Oom Flip may have drunk like a fish, but when he was sober there was no one more kind to us. Within moments, he had bandaged my brother's toe with a strip of linen ripped from a dishcloth. He even remembered to slip me a handful of pear drops, my favorite treat in all the world.

"How's your ma?" he asked. "Still no trouble from the khaki scum, I hope?"

"No, Oom."

"She's been lucky." He wrapped Ma's tobacco in brown paper and handed the bundle to me. "Word has it the commando's had a hell of a time keeping the Tommies to the ridge. The day the British Lion gets us in his sights –"

"Pa said lions are a damned nuisance," I told him.

Oom Flip roared with laughter. "You take that tobacco back to your ma with Flip's best regards," he said. "Tell her to make it last – there won't be any more until the khakis reopen the railway line from Jo'burg."

When we arrived home later that afternoon, tobacco in hand, my mother greeted us with a shriek of panic.

"What happened?" she demanded, hastening to untie the makeshift bandage that Oom Flip had wrapped around my brother's toe. At the sight of dried blood, she drew her breath sharply. "What did you do to him?"

Gert brandished the arrowhead from his pocket, narrowly slicing my mother's ear. "Look, Ma! I'm going to put it on a string and wear it around my neck like a Zulu warrior –"

"It could have been anything," continued my mother, ignoring my brother's excited chatter even while she pressed him to her chest. "The khakis might have left poisoned pieces of metal for us to step on, to infect the herds. Why weren't you paying closer attention?"

I stared at her, not knowing what to say. *You sent us,* I thought. *It's your fault we were on the Highveld.*

"She was telling me a story about Ntombazi," interjected Gert.

My mother grabbed me by the arm and shook me roughly. "More lies!" she shouted. "Heathen lies! We'll see how fit you are to spin tales once I've beaten the devil out of you –"

I wrenched myself out of her grasp, twisting my arm so hard that I felt my shoulder pop, and ran as fast as I could toward the *koppie* where my father lay buried.

"You can think twice before coming back, my girl!" Ma shouted after me, her voice cracking through the dusty air. When I glanced over my shoulder, I saw that she was clutching Gertie to her skirts, weeping soundlessly while my brother continued to admire his little stone treasure.

THE WHITE TRIBE

Just six weeks before my father died, a consumption virus had been discovered in some dead buffalo on Samie's Kloof. By the time my mother had gathered enough marula bark to make a poultice for the fever, Pa's neck had swollen to such a size that he found it difficult to turn his head. Bluish abscesses formed beneath his jaw, stretching and tautening as his neck glands expanded – until at last the skin started to rupture. The doctor said that it was scrofula, but by that point having a name for the sickness made little difference: my father had shrunk to a shadow, the purple circles under his eyes scooping hollows in his handsome face.

As Hansie was only a few months old at the time, he was the first one to be isolated. Within a few days, the doctor said that it would be best if Gert and I went to stay with Hansie at a neighboring farm. The next thing I knew, we were standing atop a *koppie* with my mother and Tant Minna, murmuring prayers over a mound of freshly turned earth.

That evening, the evening my mother shouted at me not to come home, I returned to the *koppie* where Pa was buried. Two years had passed since President Kruger declared war on the British, and already Pa's name was starting to wear from the makeshift headstone.

Morne Andries Roux
17 Februarie 1859 – 22 Desember 1899

The slate was badly chipped and had begun to crumble and flake at the corners. Someone had scratched a line through the words that our farmhand had carved with Pa's horn-handled knife – someone, perhaps, who believed the rumor that my father had wished to make peace with the British. In the early days of the war between the Boer republics and Britain, all Boer men had sworn that they would never take the oath of neutrality that the British had offered us. Anyone who did would be labeled a *hensopper,* or hands-upper: a coward and traitor to the Boer cause. My father had not been a coward, but to him the safety of his family and his farm were more important than Boer pride. To some of the men in Amersfoort, however – to the ones who called themselves *Bittereinders,* because they would fight to the bitter end – this was defeatist talk.

By now, every family was affected. Fathers, brothers, and sons were all fighting on commando. My own Oom Jakob had been killed in the raid at Mafeking. Soon, Gertie would be old enough to go and fight with my cousins, some of whom were only ten when their families sent them out into the bush with a rifle and enough ammunition to last several days. One of them, a lad of twelve named Tjaart who I'd sat with in school, had been killed after only a week. These days, the elders spoke of him as a hero, even though as far as I could remember there hadn't ever been anything remarkable about him in life. The mythology that grew up around Tjaart was bigger than he ever could have conjured up on his own had he lived. The men used it to buttress their spirits, to put fire in their bellies.

I was sure that if my father was still alive, he would be fighting with them.

The grave was piled high with rocks, and I added another stone to the mound before crouching on the soft earth. Closing my eyes, I tried not to think of the day of the funeral: the way the coffin had lurched back and forth on the shoulders of four local men who were too old and frail to be on commando and who were barely strong enough to support even my father's wasted body.

Try as I might to summon a picture of my father's healthy face, the image of the lurching coffin would not go away – so at last I opened my eyes and focused instead on the tombstone. I remembered my father chopping wood outside our house, splitting great logs into kindling, and telling me that the word *splinter* was the same in English as in Dutch. I liked the mystery of English words, the way the sounds were crisp and clean, not guttural. I used to roll them around in my mouth, savoring the thrill of speaking the enemy's tongue. Besides the names that no one could escape in those days – Queen Victoria, Lord Kitchener – the only English words I knew were *gold, farm,* and *church.*

Those were the words that summed up the history of my country. Two hundred years before I was born, French, Dutch, and German settlers fleeing religious persecution in Europe had sought a free life in southern Africa. They worked as farmers and worshipped at Dutch Reformed churches. They became known as Afrikaners and were the first of two white tribes to settle the land.

The second tribe was British, and they fought us for control of the gold mines, land, and Africans. The war that had broken out just weeks before my father died was supposed to see off the British for good – hence its name, *Tweede Vryheidsoorlog:* the Second War of Liberation.

So far, apart from food shortages and a visible absence of men, life had continued as normal in our corner of the Transvaal. Tonight, as a warm wind blew in from the east, all I could hear was the lonely clattering of a windmill from across the veld.

Tucking my legs beneath me, I curled up on the heather and folded one arm under my head. I tried to imagine my father lying deep in the earth beside me, tried to imagine the steady rise and fall of his chest, the way his mouth pulled downward when he slept. I imagined threading my arm through his, squeezing it gently as I used to when we would sit together on the veranda, counting the stars late into the night.

I fell asleep.

Sipho discovered me the next morning, curled around my father's tombstone like a cat.

"*Kleinnooi?*"

As he squatted beside me, I was aware of his bony kneecaps, his bare toes digging into the earth for balance.

"Eh?" I sat up and brushed the dirt from my shift, embarrassed by his presence. Sipho continued to stare at me, full lips parted but speechless. The whites of his eyes had turned yellow in the corners. Long eyelashes curled up toward a high, smooth forehead.

"You slept outside, *kleinnooi,* all night?"

"I'm fine, Sipho." As I made a motion to stand, he leaped up and offered me his hand.

"Hungry, *kleinnooi?*"

I nodded, and Sipho cocked his head toward home.

The servants' huts were located on the far side of the *koppie,* overlooking the scrubland where they kept a few goats and chickens. Sipho was the only son of my father's farmhand, Bheka, who had joined my uncles on commando over a year ago. Like me, Sipho had been left behind with his mother and two younger siblings – twin girls, Nosipho and Nelisiwe.

Most Boer children grew up with a *matie,* an African playmate. Sipho had been gifted to me two weeks after I was born, when he was six months old. His father called my father *baas,* and Pa called him Bheka; if Pa hadn't known his name, he would simply have called him *kaffir,* which was what we usually called a black person.

While my parents directed the labors of Sipho's parents, Sipho and I played at being equals. We dug grooves in the ground and used dried beans to play *oware,* or we gathered our siblings for a game of *mbube, mbube,* where one of us would pretend to be a lion stalking impala. Sipho showed me how to track animals by looking for fresh droppings and disturbed bush, and how to read the direction and speed of hoofprints in the dust. He taught me the difference between the curving marks left by a puff adder and a mamba, and how to recognize the spitting bugs that could blind a man with their acid saliva. He said that we needed only to listen to the earth, because it spoke better sense than most men, most of the time. He told me about the San tribesmen who hunted kudu over many days, staking their prey by outrunning it, and about the glorious victories of old. When the river was high we would fish, and when the sun grew too hot we would explore the nearby caves, which were decorated with ancient paintings. I told Sipho about Piet Reteif, the Boer leader who made a covenant with God and saved hundreds of Boer lives at the Battle of Blood River, and Sipho told me about Shaka, the warrior who united all the Zulu tribes under one banner and used a buffalo-horn formation to defeat Europeans armed with guns and canons.

Now that we were getting older, my mother said that it wasn't proper for me to spend so much time with Sipho. Soon the games of *oware* and *mbube, mbube* would have to come to an end, as would the fishing trips, tracking, and storytelling. If the war carried on much longer, Sipho would have to go and fight as a loyal African, as his father before him.

Sipho's mother was sitting in front of their thatched hut, pounding mealie corn when we arrived. Her head was wrapped in a blue cloth, and her molasses-smooth skin glistened with sweat. Seeing us, she stopped to shield her eyes from the glare of the sun and beckoned us inside. The walls were made of clay and the floor of packed earth, so the hut was cool and dark. They had only two rooms – one for cooking and eating, and one for sleeping – but it felt comfortable to me. There were no preserve jars to break, no shoes to remember, no crocheting or needlework to practice. Just a stove and some straw mattresses, and a tankard of *dop* left behind by the men.

Before I could stop him, Sipho had told his mother about my night on the gravesite. Lindiwe clicked her tongue and removed the wool blanket from her own shoulders and wrapped it around me. The coarse blanket smelled of sweet smoke and roasted corn. She then turned to the pot on the stove, and tipped the contents into two bowls.

"Eat," she said. "Eat, *kleinnooi.*"

Soft clumps of rice had settled at the bottom of the bowl, which was filled with thin porridge. I took a sip. Then another. All at once, warmth filled my mouth and throat, at last reaching my empty stomach like a spear.

"*Dankie,* Lindy," I said. Lindiwe smiled broadly, exposing teeth the color of ivory tusks, and began to untie the knotted ribbon from my hair.

"Does your ma know you were out all night?" she asked in isiZulu, combing her fingers through the matted bits.

I shrugged.

"She's angry," murmured Sipho. He knew that confronting an elephant in musth was only slightly less frightening than facing Ma when she was in one of her rages.

"*Ja-nee.*"

Lindiwe grunted. "*Ja-nee,* yes-no. That's not an answer, *kleinnooi.*" She began to twist my hair into plaits, humming a low melody until words began to form. "*Likhona ithemba, likhona kuye, thembela kuye, thembela kuJesu . . .*"

I wriggled on the mat. "Not a Jesus song, Lindy. Something else."

Sipho looked up, grinning, from his porridge.

"*O bring my t'rug na die ou Transvaal, Daar waar my Sarie woon . . .*"

I couldn't help but join in. "*Daar onder in die mielies, By die groen doringboom, Daar woon my Sarie Marais . . .*" We'd learned the song from a couple of men who'd recently returned from Pretoria, where it had become popular among the Boer commandos.

> O take me back to the old Transvaal
> where my Sarie lives,
> Down among the maize fields near the green thorn
> tree,
> there lives my Sarie Marais . . .

Lindiwe pulled a face and shook her head, waggling her hands at us. "So much noise, you two! Go, now – out, out. Take these." She passed us two small loaves of mealie bread and a few shriveled strips of biltong, suddenly looking very serious. "Wrap the bread and meat in the blanket and leave them in the pigeon lofts for the men, *kleinnooi*. Albert Siswe said that their supplies are running low again."

I considered the meager bundle. "No salt?"

Lindiwe stared down at her palms, shaking her head slowly. "Your ma sent coffee and sugar two weeks ago – there was no salt then, either."

I heaved the bundle under one arm and tried to sound cheery. "Never mind – things are getting better.

Soon, the Transvaal and the Free State will be just that: free. You'll see." I grabbed Sipho's hand and tugged him out the door. "*Totsiens,* Lindy."

The pigeon lofts were on Tant Minna's land, near the edge of the Lowveld where the herds grazed in winter. As Sipho and I followed the trickling stream that divided the Highveld from the foothills, I could tell that my friend's mind was elsewhere.

"Things aren't getting better," he said solemnly. "The commandos are outnumbered."

"Don't say that," I snapped. "We won at Colenso, didn't we? And at Spion Kop. You could hear the pom-poms firing from the ridge." I strode on ahead, irritated by my friend's silence. "Pa used to say, 'There's no better horseman or marksman in the world than a Boer' – and he was right, too. My uncles blew up two telegraph sites last month, and your pa was there when they raided the storage depot – "

"That was in the spring. It's different now."

I kicked at a stone in stride and shifted the bundle of food from one arm to the other. "That's not what the generals say. De Wet isn't giving up." I turned around and prodded my companion in the ribs. "*Our great General Christiaan de Wet / Is still too small for the khaki net.* Remember that, Sipho?"

Sipho only grunted.

As we rounded the bluffs overlooking Tant Minna's farm, I felt Sipho's fingers snap to my shoulder. "Listen," he said. "Do you hear that?" He began to kneel slowly, reaching for a sharp-edged stone by my feet, his gaze trained straight ahead.

"Is it kudu?" Sipho may have been a crack-shot with a rifle, but I couldn't imagine him felling a large animal with a rock.

"Get down."

Sipho had never spoken to me like that before, and at first I was too affronted to do anything. Then I saw the fear in his eyes, the way his brown irises seemed to tremble in their yellow-white sea, and I too sank to the ground.

"There," whispered Sipho. "Do you see?"

From where we crouched, I could just make out one of the slatted pigeon lofts. Wildflowers and weeds sprouted brazenly around the hut, bending in the breeze that whisked sprays of sand against its walls. The corrugated metal roof glinted in the sun.

"What?"

Sipho yanked me closer, forced my head at an angle. "Look."

The door to the loft was open, creaking on a rusty hinge.

Before either of us could say anything more, two figures appeared from the open loft, shoulders hunched, heads craned forward through the low doorway. They wore cream trousers that were loose from the hip to the knee, but from knee to ankle the fabric was wrapped tightly with beige puttees. Brass buttons gleamed on starched jackets; laced boots had been buffed to a high shine. One of the men carried a domed helmet in the crook of his arm.

Khakis.

I glanced at Sipho, who was turning the rock between his fingers. I could tell that he was thinking of throwing it to create a distraction. If the English soldiers discovered the supplies that we had been hiding for our commandos, they would raze every Boer house for miles around.

Then, just as he was beginning to raise his arm, Sipho froze. We had both noticed the same thing: the package of clothes that we'd left beneath one of the beams in a dark corner of the loft, covered with straw, now lay piled on the open ground behind the house. They had already discovered the hiding place.

"Come, *kleinnooi* – we can't stay," hissed Sipho.

"Wait." I wanted to see these men, to know their faces. I had never been this close to a British soldier before. One of the men was young, with bowlegs and a shock of red hair. The older one was taller, more solidly built, with black hair combed to the side and a neat black mustache. They were talking, but even if we understood English it would have been difficult to make out the words.

Sipho had already begun his silent retreat. I gathered the bundle of food together and wondered where we might leave it in case there were hungry commandos waiting nearby. The pigeon lofts would be off limits even after the British soldiers had left. The khakis would interrogate Tant Minna and see to it that all the outbuildings were destroyed . . .

"Please, *kleinnooi*. Come!"

Stealing one last glance at the soldiers, I followed Sipho into the long grass.

A PILLAR OF SALT

I arrived home to find my mother shelling peas outside the house, her face obscured by a peaked cap. The days were now so hot that even raindrops would sizzle as they hit the dry earth. Ma must have been stewing under her gingham dress – but if any woman was going to preserve decorum in that terrible heat, she would. My brothers, both in states of undress, crouched at her feet: Gert was showing Hansie the bushman arrow that now hung from a leather cord around his neck.

It was almost a happy scene, and I was about to ruin it.

"Where have you been?" demanded my mother as she tipped the pea shells from her apron into a shallow bowl.

"Sipho and I saw khakis at Tant Minna's," I blurted. "Coming out of the pigeon lofts."

I'd sent Sipho back to his mother with the bundle of food. At least until the khakis had gone, it seemed best not to risk drawing attention to ourselves. If there were any commandos waiting in the bush, they'd have to go hungry for another day.

"Minna's?" The lines in my mother's forehead seemed to deepen, and what little color there was in her face quickly drained from her cheeks, turning her gray as a stone. "If this is another story, Corlie Roux –"

"You can ask Sipho. They found the clothes we'd left for the men."

"How many were there?"

"Just two."

"And Minna?"

"We didn't see her." They'd be setting fire to the house by now, herding my aunt and my cousins onto cattle wagons . . .

"Andries? Danie?"

I shook my head.

"Did they see you?"

"No, Ma."

We'd heard the stories of women and children who had been dragged from their houses even as they begged the British for mercy. If they were lucky, they would be given a few minutes to remove any valuables before the entire farm was set alight. *Scorched earth,* the British called it: destroying everything of their enemies – livestock, crops, food stores – so that there was no way they could sustain commandos in the bush. Then, the British poisoned the wells and salted the fields so that the *Boere* would not be able to begin again.

My mother was silent. She considered the fields, studded with prickly pear, and then she turned and stared up at our house. Pressing the back of her hand to her mouth, she turned toward the fields again. For a long time, she seemed torn between two unspeakable thoughts. Then, with an almost violent assurance that made it seem as if there had never been any doubt in her mind, she grabbed each of my brothers by the arm and pushed them inside.

"We'll join the *laager*," she said to me. "We won't wait for them to come to us."

"But the *laager*'s miles away," I protested. Weeks ago, we had been asked if we wanted to join the company of families that were going to live in wagons on the veld, moving every few days to keep out of the enemy's sights. "We'll never find them —"

"I'm not staying here to see everything destroyed," hissed my mother. I recognized the growing hysteria in her voice and clamped my mouth shut. "Put on everything you can wear, and then go and tell Lindy to bring the children."

"Yes, Ma."

In our bedroom, Gert watched me roll on three pairs of stockings until I could barely squeeze my feet into my boots. I reached for a pair of socks that was draped over the back of a chair and pointed to the heavy leather shoes in the corner.

"Put those on, Gertie," I said, trying to control the tremor in my voice.

"I don't want to wear shoes," he said softly.

"Put them on," I told him. "We'll have to walk a long way." He continued to stand there, wide-eyed, and so I paused from helping Hansie to give Gertie a shove. "And find a shirt. A jacket, too. Roll up the blankets."

My brother did as he was told, then disappeared into the other room for a few moments before returning with my father's hat. It was far too large for Gertie; trying it on, his face disappeared beneath the wide, floppy brim.

"I want Pa to come."

"Pa can't come. Don't be *dom*."

"I'm going to bring his hat, then. I don't want the khakis burning his hat."

I stopped trying to stuff Hansie's chubby legs into his breeches and looked up at my brother. He was fingering the arrowhead absently, twisting the leather cord as far as it would go before starting to turn it in the opposite direction.

"Do you know where Pa's coat is?"

"*Ja,* with the hat."

"Bring it here."

For once, he did not argue but came straight back with my father's calfskin coat. The leather was as soft as felt, and it smelled of sweet grass. I pulled it on and rolled up the sleeves. The pockets reached down past my knees.

"*Goed.*" I glanced about our room, taking in all the little details that had never seemed terribly important: a wash-stand with china jug and basin, my unfinished embroidery sampler, a plant pot decoupaged with images of the cathedral in Ghent, the skittles that Oom Jakob had carved for my brother. "Fetch as many rusks as you can fit in your pockets. Biltong, too. Fruit will only spoil –"

"Are you still here?" My mother had appeared in the doorway, Pa's rifle slung over one shoulder. "It's time you fetched Lindy and the children – Gert can help me with Hansie."

"Yes, Ma."

When Sipho saw me – dwarfed by my father's coat, wool stockings bunching out of my boots, twin petti-coats rustling under my smock – he made no attempt to hide his surprise.

"Playing dress up, *kleinnooi?* Haven't you told your ma about the khakis?"

"We're going to join the *laager,* Sipho. You must get your sisters ready quickly – we're leaving as soon as we can."

My friend looked as if he might say something, but then he seemed to think better of it. We had known this day would come, sooner or later: either we would have to join the *laager,* or watch our farm go up in flames. There wasn't time to be afraid. After all, this was what Boer women and children had been prepared for since the war started; this is what made us strong – my father had said so himself. I wasn't about to let him down.

Sipho bolted into the hut. Seconds later, Lindiwe emerged, supporting Nelisiwe on one hip and Nosipho on the other.

"What's this, *kleinnooi?*"

"Ma doesn't want to be here when the khakis come. They'll be searching all the houses in the area –"

"*Aiyoh* . . ." Lindiwe handed Nelisiwe to Sipho. "There's mealie *pap* in the pot, and *morogo* from last night. Can we take the chickens?"

I shook my head, not daring to meet her in the eye. Lindy doted on her chickens as if they were her own children. Her favorite was Mbaba Mwana, a silky hen with full feather pantaloons and a cat's purr.

"Not even the goat? Nothing?"

"There will be animals at the *laager*," I said lamely. "We can leave some corn out for Mbaba Mwana . . ."

But Lindy had already steeled herself, was busily retying her headscarf: a sure sign that there was work to be done. "Don't worry about Mbaba Mwana, *kleinnooi*. She's only a chicken. We must get you all away from here. That's the important thing . . ."

Sipho and I were put in charge of essentials: filling the paraffin lamp, pouring milk into skin sacks, secreting what food we could into the folds of our clothes. Duly laden with provisions, we returned to the house to collect my mother and brothers. As we waited in the kitchen, considering all the things that we would have to leave behind, I noticed Sipho staring at the knife my mother used for gutting fish.

"For protection, *kleinnooi*." He picked it up, ran one finger along the mean edge.

"But we have the rifle."

"A rifle is only useful as long as we have bullets." Sipho reached for the muslin cloth that Ma used for steaming puddings and began to wrap it around the blade, a makeshift sheath. "Just in case. No need to worry, *kleinnooi*." His gaze drifted around the kitchen, and for the first time I saw the room through his eyes: the uselessness of my mother's lace curtains, the crocheted tablecloth, the decorative milk glass plates.

"*Aanjaag*," I said. "Let's go."

The sky was streaked yellow and pink as we guided the carriage off the main road and into the bush. Our mule's sides heaved like bellows as I urged her on, slapping my bonnet against her bony haunches while Ma tugged at the reins with clenched fists. My brothers and Lindiwe's little girls balanced atop our piled belongings, wide-eyed and silent, while Lindiwe and Sipho pushed from behind. No one spoke.

As we walked, I thought about the soldier with the black mustache – the way he had nudged the pile of clothes with one toe, hands on hips, shaking his head as if he'd just discovered the dead body of a beloved dog. Watching him, I hadn't been frightened. And yet here I was now, trying to read my mother's expression as she chewed grimly on her pipe, my heart drumming a tattoo through my chest. We had left everything — the sheep, the goat, the chickens — and we were walking into darkness. I pulled my father's coat more tightly around my shoulders, and gave the donkey another whop with my bonnet.

Ma seemed to think that the *laager* had moved on toward Standerton, so we followed the sun west across the *platteland*, keeping our eyes peeled for wagon tracks. When we had been going for almost two hours, Ma decreed that we should set up camp by some bushes that had a good view of the veld. Lindiwe unloaded the heavy iron pot to prepare a brew of red-bush tea, and Gert set about collecting pieces of dry bracken for a fire. My mother passed me a bucket and told me to fetch water from the stream, which lay about half a mile away. All afternoon we had been traveling parallel to it, just as the *laager* would.

"Don't go as far as Samie's Kloof," she said. "The khakis might be using it as a lookout. It will be dark in an hour, so make sure you're back before then."

"I'll go, too," volunteered Sipho.

"No," said my mother. She pointed to the tarpaulin at the back of the carriage. "You'll help me to create a shelter, Sipho. Gertie isn't strong enough to plant the stakes."

"Yes, *nooi*." Sipho lowered his eyes and scurried around to the back of the carriage. My mother shot me a look, which I pretended to ignore as I slung the bucket over one shoulder.

I reached the stream in no time at all, and realized that our little party, encumbered by the carriage, supplies, three small children, and a geriatric donkey, had moved far more slowly than if I had walked the same distance alone. It occurred to me that if I hurried, I might make it up to Samie's Kloof in time to find out if the khakis had reached our house. Casting a quick glance over my shoulder to make sure that no one would see me, I dropped the bucket by some rocks in the shallows and crept upstream. Then, keeping to the tree line, I broke into a sprint. I told myself that I was like the solitary *sengi* shrew, which depends on its speed for survival and can run almost as soon as it is born.

When I reached the ridge, it soon became clear that I was not the first to have passed this way in recent days. Carriage tracks followed the rutted trail that skirted the Kloof, and the air buzzed with flies hovering around fresh horse droppings. But whoever had come through here hadn't pitched camp; the convoy of vehicles and people must have been aiming for the group of farms not two miles from where I stood.

Crouching on all fours, I scrambled up the ridge to the point where the earth evened out and offered a plain view of the valley below. There, just below the horizon, was our whitewashed little house: low-slung and circled by a wire fence, with a line of washing strung out the back and a smattering of wildflowers brightening the parched yard. I lay down, and from here it was possible to make out the movement of several black dots trailing about the porch: Lindiwe's chickens, almost certainly. And then I realized that what should have been there – the goat that we'd left tethered to its post – wasn't.

My thoughts began to race as I noticed more problems with the scene. What had happened to the sheep? Where was the dairy cow we had kept on when Ma sold our herds after Pa died? They should have been in the field, where there was still grazing to be had. I squinted into the distance, wondering if perhaps they had broken rank and fled when they realized that we were not coming back.

And that was when I saw it: a plume of smoke rising from behind the house like the puff of licorice tobacco that grew out of my mother's pipe. But this smoke didn't divide into tendrils, twisting and curling in the breeze; it spread like ink seeping through water, staining the sky black. Seconds later, I smelled something sickly sweet, something rotten: a burning smell, different from wood fire or coal.

Then I knew what had become of our goat and our sheep and our dairy cow, and my stomach tightened.

All at once, I felt myself filling up with the desire to yell, to wave my hands and shout at those dumb chickens so that they might make one last, desperate attempt at flight. *Go!* I wanted to say. *Get away from there while you can! Go, Mbaba Mwana. Go and be free!*

But in an instant I realized that the chickens were of little interest to the men who had slaughtered our livestock, the soldiers who even now were dragging our

kitchen table through the front door. I watched help-
lessly as they returned for Ma's dresser and Pa's rifle
trunk, as well as for all four kitchen chairs, which my
father had built himself. Everything went on a pile in the
yard. They moved quickly, tossing bags of mealie corn
and cured meat through the smashed windows, unscrew-
ing jars of preserves and digging out pieces of fruit with
their fingers. One of them came out with an open box
that belched clothing, trailing my mother's stockings
and a pair of breeches that belonged to Gert. These
they tossed onto the furniture pile. Someone threw my
brother's fiddle at the growing mountain, and I imagined
the crack of split wood, the snapping of wire strings.

Knowing what was to come next, I wanted to turn
away – and yet I couldn't bring myself to move. I watched
one of the men light and raise a torch, then set the
whole lot on fire. I continued to watch as a second
plume of smoke rose higher and higher into the air
until it joined with the first one, smearing the sky with
the remains of our modest home. I felt myself fill with
rage – a fury that made my temples pound and my eyes
burn – and still I watched.

I watched, and I did nothing.

When I could bear it no longer, I pushed up onto my
elbows and began to steer myself back down the ridge –
away from the gruesome stench, away from the pitiful
destruction and ugly insult to the life my parents had
built for us. *Don't look back,* I told myself. *Remember what
happened to Lot's wife. She looked back, and she turned into a*

pillar of salt. Don't look back.

And then I saw him: a lone figure standing on the periphery of the farm not twenty yards from the edge of the kloof. He must have been supervising the sack of our house without bothering to dirty his own hands. He stood in profile, and I could make out the curve of his mustache, the waxed sweep of black hair.

Don't look back.

It was too late. The soldier turned in my direction and his eyes locked with mine. For a moment we both froze, existing only in each other's gaze. From where I was, it was just possible to make out the shape of the badge on his jacket – it looked like a leaf – and as I tried to muster the courage to scream, I focused on that badge, wondering what it meant.

The soldier squinted up at me, and his mouth opened slightly as if he might have said something to me – not to anyone else, as there was no one near enough to hear him – before steeling his jaw and turning the other way. I waited for him to shout to the others, to raise the alarm – *Boer spies on the ridge! Take aim, men!* – but he did nothing. For several seconds I waited, hardly daring to breathe.

And then, the strangest thing of all happened: he looked at me again, and he moved his head as if to say, *Go. Go while you can.*

I ran all the way to the campsite, stopping only to fill the bucket, and I didn't look back once.

THE GREAT TREK

Not for the first time, we turned our backs on the world.

Ma said we were no different from the women and children who had endured the trials of the Great Trek in my grandparents' day, living by their wits off the earth that God had given them. Like those women and children, we depended on African knowledge to survive. Lindiwe knew which bushes grew leaves that could be stripped and boiled for broth, and which ones were better suited for kindling. Sipho knew how to trace the curve of the Vaal River simply by judging the contours of the yellow sandstone hills. With their knowledge, we could have continued roaming like that for weeks. Ma knew this as well as I, but that didn't make her grateful: she was far too proud to admit that we would surely have died without their help.

I once made the mistake of asking Ma if it was true that an African tribe in the Transkei could trace its descent to a white woman. I remembered one of Pa's friends telling us that European sailors shipwrecked off the Cape centuries ago found they had no choice but to join local clans in order to survive. That's why sometimes you would hear of Afrikaner children being born the wrong color – *throwbacks,* they were called – because black blood could be held in store for many generations.

"Does that mean I could have black blood?" I asked Ma hopefully. "Does that make me properly African, like Sipho?"

My mother didn't answer yes or no: she only smacked me for my impudence, and told me to see that Hansie didn't need changing.

We'd heard stories of Boer women who had tried to talk their husbands into surrendering, because *laager* life in wartime was just too hard. "How long did they think we could outlast the khakis?" those women would ask. "The khakis, with their guns and their horses and their endless stream of supplies brought in from all corners of the mighty British Empire?" But in a strange way, my mother seemed to enjoy hardship. She thrived off it. The only story I had ever heard her tell with any pleasure was of the time that old Karel Snyman returned home after becoming separated from his commando in a skirmish. His wife, a battle-ax known to us children as *de Bul,* had opened the door, taken one look at her husband with an expression of pure disgust, and said,

"Back to the front, you coward . . . and don't come home without our country's freedom!"

Ma would break into howls of laughter at this, but I knew she would have said the same to Pa if he had shirked his duty. Ma took to heart the expected responsibilities of a Boer woman: raising her children in the true faith and staunchly enduring whatever was demanded of her by the men who led us. She was like a mother cheetah, an animal that raises her cubs single-handedly, without any help from a pack. My mother didn't ask questions, and she expected me to do the same.

On the third morning, Lindiwe told Ma that we had finished the last of the meat and *morogo* leaves. The night before, Ma had made *potjiekos* with some poached chicken that wasn't going to last another day. The beef *wors* and biltong were also gone. All that was left was a knot of giblets, a few spices, some mealie flour, and a jar of peaches.

"We'll make do," said Ma. "We'll have porridge and tea tonight. We'll catch up with the *laager* by tomorrow."

Tomorrow came and went, and still there was no sign of the *laager*.

By the sixth day, we had traveled almost as far as Standerton. Our mule's distended belly heaved against its rib cage with long, rattling sighs that reminded us of our own hunger. We were all growing tired of the porridge, which seemed to grow thinner at each meal, so when Ma suggested sending Sipho on ahead to barter for supplies in the town, my friend leaped to his feet as fast as a blesbok.

"Yes, *nooi!*"

"Let me go, too," I said, watching him stalk off.

"Don't be silly," said my mother. Tiny beads of sweat dotted her upper lip, which had tightened into a thin line. "Do you want to give us away? No one will notice a *kaffir* alone, but if he's spotted walking into town with a white girl the khakis will seek us out faster than you can blink." She withdrew a couple of wire hooks from the folds of her skirt and passed them to me. "While Sipho's gone, you can take your *boetie* down to the river and catch something for dinner. Collect groundnuts if the fish aren't biting."

"I'm too hot," said Gert irritably.

"We can swim in the river," I told him.

"You will do no such thing," Ma snapped. "No dawdling, no games. Either you come back with food for this evening, or you don't come back at all."

"Yes, Ma."

The land here was greener than the desolate veld we had left behind us. Tiny sugarbirds buzzed over the clusters of pink heather that grew between the rocks on gently sloping *koppies*. Somewhere in the distance, a lourie bird cried out to its mate.

"I thought we weren't supposed to pick wild nuts," mused Gert, concentrating on the ground as he walked a few paces in front of me. The back of his neck had turned brown in the sun, offsetting the fine golden hairs on his nape. "Ma always said we'd get a beating if she found out we'd eaten from the bush. *Optelgoed is jakkalspiepie.*"

I allowed myself to smile. How many times had she told us that picked-up things were no better than jackal's pee? But that had been before we'd become homeless, before foraging had become a way of life. Lindiwe had shown us which plants were poisonous and which ones were safe. Anything we didn't recognize, we wouldn't eat.

We continued in silence, pausing only to watch a goshawk slice between the treetops on its afternoon death-cruise. When we reached the riverbank, I tore off a thread from the hem of my dress and showed Gert how to tie it onto a fishhook. We gathered sticks for rods, and used bright protea leaves for bait. Then we slipped our dry-soled feet into the sparkling water and waited, trying to ignore our growling stomachs.

"Tell me the story about the sea serpent," said Gert after a while.

I thought hard, studying the rippling stream as it tripped and gurgled over the rocks. Neither of us had ever seen the sea. Ma had read to us about the Sea of Galilee in the Bible, and Tant Minna had taught us to color the ocean blue in the maps we drew for geography lessons. Sometimes I would dream that I was standing on a beach, listening to the soft rush of frothing waves, feeling the fresh breeze blow through my hair and the crunch of the salty air between my teeth. Once I had boasted to Gert that I intended to run away and become a lady pirate.

He had only laughed, but I knew better; after all, the ocean was wild and free, abounding with possibilities.

"Not long ago," I began, "some fishermen discovered a carcass washed up on the shore. They could tell that it had been there for quite a long time, because the bones had bleached in the sun, and most of the skin –"

"What color was the skin?"

"Shiny, black-green skin, with whiskers as coarse as elephant hair." I smiled. "Most of it had dried up completely. One of the men thought it might have been a whale, but they had seen whales before and this wasn't the right shape. Another man said it might have been a large python, but no one had seen a python of this size before. Then a little boy – the youngest son of one of the fishermen – noticed something very strange . . ."

I stared off into the undergrowth on the opposite bank, trying to decide what the little boy could have noticed about the creature. A golden tooth? The remains of some other animal deep inside its belly? Something else rising out of the water? And then, just as I had decided on the perfect twist, I saw him.

The black-haired man.

He was dragging something through the bush, breathing heavily from the exertion. Noticing my silence, Gert turned to look at me and then followed my gaze. We both watched, too frightened to move, as the soldier lumbered toward us.

There would have been time to run – the man was on the other side of the riverbank, after all – but the sound of something so heavy being pulled across the ground made a hundred gruesome thoughts rush into my head. Perhaps it was a body – the dead body of a Boer woman whose house had been gutted by the khakis. Or perhaps it was one of our men, a commando who had fallen in battle or been murdered in his sleep. Perhaps the soldier was going to hide the body, or throw it in the river, or worse –

"Look, Corlie!"

When the deadweight shape came into view, I had to bite the inside of my mouth to keep from making any noise.

It was a springbok – male, judging by the short, thick antlers, but quite young. Its golden tan coat was glossy and smooth, but its white belly was stained with blood. It was difficult to see where the gaping tear ended and the dark brown stripe of fur began, but it was clear that the animal was long dead. The soldier was hauling it by the legs, so the animal's silky neck lolled to one side. For a brief moment, it seemed to stare at me with one wide, black eye.

"Come on, Gert," I whispered. "Be very quiet. Get up, slowly, and follow me . . ."

It was too late. As soon as the rustling ceased, I knew that the soldier had seen us. For an instant, the black-haired man looked almost as scared as we felt. Then he smiled, and pointed to the dead springbok.

"Lions got him," he said. "He must have been heading down to the river for a drink – just like I was – when they

· attacked him." Although I couldn't understand his words, I knew that he was speaking English.

"Don't say anything," I told Gert. The soldier didn't appear to have any gun, and the river formed a safe barrier between us: we could still outrun him.

The black-haired man's smile faded. "Lions," he said again, pointing to the ugly gash that ran across the springbok's belly. Then he stopped, as if realizing who we were, and squinted up into the sun, thinking hard.

"*Leeu,*" he said at last. "Lions."

My brother fixed me with a terrified look. "Lions, Corlie," he said. "Ma didn't say there were lions about —"

"Sh!"

The black-haired man gently lowered the animal's legs to the ground, and then he stood up straight, in full view. He eyed me up and down, wiping his hands on his trousers.

"I've seen you before," he said, pulling the back of his hand across his brow. He wore a wide-brimmed hat that looked a bit like the kind our men favored, different from the English soldiers' domed helmets. "You're the little girl from the farm back Amersfoort way."

Gert looked up at me. "What's he saying, Corlie?"

"I don't know."

The black-haired man knelt by the water and began to wash his hands.

"Boer kids, are you?"

Gert nodded at the word *Boer*, and I thumped him.

The black-haired man smiled. "You've walked a long way," he said. "What are your names?"

We stared at him.

"I'm Corporal Malachi Byrne," he said. He pointed one finger at himself. "Corporal Byrne." He pointed at us. "And you?"

"Gert Roux," blurted Gertie, understanding the gestures. And, before I could stop him, "*en* Corlie Roux."

"Corlie Roux." The black-haired man said my name slowly, drawing out the vowels. "Well, pleased to meet you, Corlie Roux. That's a mighty big coat you've got on." He drew his hands up and down his sides, then pointed at my father's coat. When I realized what he was saying, I drew it more tightly around my shoulders.

"Don't get me wrong – it's a nice coat," continued the black-haired man. What had he said his name was? *Corporal Byrne*. He stroked his mustache with the finger and thumb of one hand, looking thoughtful. "Are you kids hungry? 'Cause there's no way I'm going to haul this fellow all the way back to camp." He pointed to the springbok and mimed eating.

Gert tugged at my side. "The lions will follow him, Corlie. He shouldn't drag it around like that."

Corporal Byrne drew a small knife from his belt and began to cut away at one of the haunches. The flesh was tender and yielding, pink. Suddenly, I was very hungry. "This isn't so different from the deer we get back home," he said. Then he stopped, and looked up at me. "On my farm," he said.

Farm. I knew that word.

"*Engeland,*" I said, to show him that I knew. I said the word as if it made a rotten taste in my mouth, just in case he had any doubt as to what I thought of his country.

But Corporal Byrne just laughed – a full-throated laugh, with a smile that opened up his whole face – and shook his head.

"No, not England," he said. "Alberta. Canada." He pointed to the badge that I had noticed before. "See this? It's a maple leaf. A leaf –" He pointed into the treetops, and I nodded. "Canadian Mounted Rifles." The smile faded as he returned to work. "But you're right, we're giving the Tommies a hand out here. King and Country, and all that. Seems a little crazy, now that I think about it. I've never even been to England, you know – and here I am, fighting for the English king."

We watched him deftly slice a lump of glistening flesh from the animal's side before withdrawing a handkerchief from his pocket. My brother looked up at me, gauging my reaction. At that moment, we both would have done anything for a taste of juicy buck. After days of heavily salted biltong and dry pot-bread, the thought of fresh meat was almost too much to bear.

Corporal Byrne wrapped the lump of haunch in the handkerchief and fastened the cloth together with the pin that had attached the badge to his lapel. The badge he slipped into another pocket.

"I'll tell them it fell off in the bush," he grinned. "You kids look hungry. Can you catch?" He mimed tossing the bundle across the river. "Are you ready? You, Gert – will you catch this?"

Gertie nodded.

Corporal Byrne slung the wrapped haunch through the air, and my brother lunged for it, cradling it to his chest with a grunt.

"You'd make a sharp wide receiver, Gert," smiled the soldier.

I decided that Pa would have liked Corporal Byrne. Maybe that's why, as I watched him start to gather the springbok's legs to haul him off once more, I shouted, "*Laat dit vir die leeus!*" Leave some for the lions. I knew that they would return to finish off their kill – and if they caught a human scent on it, they'd track Corporal Byrne all the way back to his camp.

He turned and stared at me. "What's that, Corlie?"

I made a growling sound, swiping at the air as if my hand had become a paw. "*Leeu,*" I said. Then I pointed at the ground.

Corporal Byrne looked down at the springbok and back up at me. At last, a look of comprehension dawned across his handsome face.

"Oh, I see," he said. "You're a clever girl, Corlie." He contemplated the springbok and withdrew his knife once more. "I guess it'll be just a couple of chops for supper, then."

We watched him butcher a leg before returning the

carcass to the bush. "Let's hope the lions don't mind my borrowing some." Then he tipped his hat at us and raised one hand in farewell. "Take care, you two. Be sure to cook that meat good and proper."

And then, just as quickly as he had appeared, he was gone.

THE ORPHAN

I told Gert to get rid of the handkerchief and the pin so that Ma wouldn't know we'd been given the meat by a khaki.

"We'll tell her that we found the buck ourselves," I said. It was clear that my brother was just as impatient as I was to bite into a hot roast. "We can say that we cut it up with the fishhooks. If she hears we spoke to a soldier, she'll use the *sjambok*." And then, just to be sure that he understood, I added, "Otherwise, I'll tell her that you were the one who gave him our names."

"I won't tell, Corlie – promise."

Ma's mouth dropped open when I presented her with the dark red lump of haunch meat.

"Where'd you find this?"

"Lions must have got him, Ma. We left the rest so they wouldn't follow us."

My mother took the flesh in both hands, feeling the fine white hairs on the side that Corporal Byrne hadn't bothered to skin.

"We'll have *sosaties* tonight," she said. "There's still some ginger jam for a sauce . . . and the last of the peaches . . ." For the first time in many weeks, I detected the glimmer of a smile on her weather-beaten face.

I couldn't remember when last I'd done something to please my mother, but that night she seemed almost happy. She told Gert she was proud of him, and although she did not say as much to me, I felt sure that I had also won some approval. I basked in her good favor all evening.

After dinner, lying beneath the wagon with Gert curled up against one side of me and Lindiwe cradling me with her body on the other, I wondered if Corporal Byrne had eaten as well as we had. Before taking my first mouthful of tender meat, it occurred to me that perhaps the buck had been poisoned, that Gert and I had fallen prey to a khaki trap. But the springbok had tasted exactly as it should: lighter than kudu or ostrich meat, and slightly sweet. I couldn't remember ever having feasted on anything so delicious.

Then, another thought: what if Corporal Byrne told his comrades about us? What if, even now, a group of khakis was scouring the riverbank for traces of the two children sighted casting for fish? Surely Gert wasn't old enough to be considered a threat; we obviously hadn't been part of any guerrilla commando. But what if they tracked us back to Ma – what would become of Sipho and Lindiwe?

These were the questions that troubled me as I drifted off to sleep, lulled by a lavender breeze and the distant cries of a lone bush baby.

"Corlie! Corlie, wake up!"

The blurry shape of my brother's arrowhead swung to and fro against a pale blue sky. I rubbed my eyes and raised myself onto my elbows, grumpily pushing Gert aside.

"What is it?" Had Corporal Byrne betrayed us after all? Were the khakis on their way?

"Sipho has found the *laager!*"

He'd sighted it a mile upstream, heading south. Apparently one of the men had recognized him as Bheka's son and told the others not to shoot.

When my mother saw Oom Sarel emerging from the bush, she let out a cry that cut through the still morning air like a jackknife.

"Sarel!" Ma flung both arms around the old man's leathery neck and planted a kiss on his cheek. I had never seen her look so happy in my life, and suddenly I realized just how frightened she had been.

"What have you been doing all the way out here, Maria?" His puckered mouth quivered into a smile as he took in the details of our feeble camp. "Surviving on flies and dew, by the looks of it. Get your boy to pack up the wagon, and I'll take you back to the *laager*. Minna will be relieved to see you."

"Minna?" My mother's hand shot to her mouth. "She's with you? And the boys?"

"They caught wind of a British column near the farm with only minutes to spare. She keeps saying she'd never forgive herself if the devils got to you. Apparently they destroyed everything." The old man spat at the ground. "Khaki scum."

"God be praised – He heard my prayers!" My mother smoothed her hair with trembling hands. "Corlie! Gert! Don't just stand there like a couple of *domkops*. Help Lindiwe with the mule, get your brother into the wagon, put out the fire – we're leaving this place."

Oom Sarel showed us the point at which we had diverged from the *laager*'s course, about two miles from where we had set up camp. "We've been keeping near to the river, where it's sheltered by the forest. We didn't want to risk pitching up by the open water," he said. I stole a look at Gert, whose forehead had puckered in thought. I could tell he was thinking about Corporal Byrne.

There were about twenty people in the *laager*, living out of four covered wagons garrisoned by a line of ebony trees. It was the largest gathering of *Boere* that I could remember seeing for many months. When Tant Minna saw us, she gathered Hansie in her arms and covered Gert's golden head with kisses. Her sons, Danie and Andries, poked their heads from their wagon to eye us warily.

"We thought you'd been eaten by lions," said Danie.

"Or arrested by the khakis," said Andries.

As they peered out at us from beneath the canvas, their eyes, ringed with dark circles, were as piercing and defensive as those of a couple of cornered foxes.

"Well, we weren't," I snapped, wishing that they wouldn't stare so. Only then did I realize how ragged I must have looked. "We ate buck meat last night."

"You didn't."

"We did!" Gert caught my eye just in time: he must have realized that if he said any more I would let him have it.

"Gert and I found it near the river. Lions got it," I said.

There was no time to discuss this any further, as Oom Sarel began to usher us toward the wagons. "There are leopards about these parts, and they hunt at night," he told us. "They'll take you for a warthog, and then you'll be sorry."

This made Gert laugh. Just a few weeks earlier, when we had been wandering through the bush near our house, my brother had stopped dead in his tracks and pointed at the pair of yellow eyes staring at us through the undergrowth. The protruding snout, heavy jowls, and curved tusks were caked in mud. Stiff bristles rose from erect, pointed ears and spine; the rest of its body was covered in thick, black fur that shimmered in the late afternoon sun. The warthog's brawny shoulders looked as powerful as a horse's hindquarters, and its breath escaped in parallel gusts from its nostrils in hot, swirling bursts. Our voices must have startled the beast, which had come to drink at the stream, and it let out something between a belch and a groan before crashing off into a thicket with its wiry, black tail flung high in the air. To my shame, I had screamed – a noise that frightened Gert even more than the creature with the yellow eyes – before realizing that the warthog was even more scared than we were. We had laughed about it all the way home.

"From now on, we stay in the *laager*," said Lindiwe. "See how the wagons make a circle, Gertie? You must not leave the circle."

"Why, Lindiwe?"

"To stay safe."

"What if we need to fetch water?" I asked.

"There's more than enough water here already," said Oom Sarel proudly. "The Van Zyls and the Cronjes brought two barrels. There's no need for anyone to go any farther than those thornbushes." He must have mistaken my look of horror for stunned relief, as he pulled one sinewy arm around my shoulders and smiled, chucking me gently under the chin. "You'll be well looked after from now on, Corlie Roux. There's four of us men here in the *laager,* so no need for the womenfolk to fret. Go help your ma with that little brother of yours. There's a good girl."

From what I could tell, the four men Oom Sarel had mentioned were all at least as old as he. It shouldn't have come as any surprise – no local man under the age of sixty would be caught dead cowering in the bush with women and children – but it didn't make me feel any safer. To be the only girl in a *laager* of men and boys: now that would have been a great accomplishment. But to be just one of many girls and women, who had no choice but to defer to their elders, was simply humiliating.

Besides Tant Minna and my cousins, the other families were from farms on the other side of Amersfoort. They watched us silently from between fluttering canvas curtains, no doubt judging how much we'd eat into their rations. Would there be enough to feed our family and Lindiwe's? And for how long?

I wandered up to my mother, who was still chattering excitedly with Tant Minna and another woman who I recognized as the local midwife.

"Ma, I need to pee," I said. "Can I go to the bushes?"

My mother looked at me distractedly. "Do you need to ask me before doing anything, Corlie?" she snapped. Then she turned back to the other women to ask how long the meat had been drying in the wind, and how many loaves of ash bread they could bake in the communal fire.

It was precisely the permission I had been hoping for.

We'd not been in the *laager* for half an hour, and already I was feeling suffocated by the swarm of half-starved children, the exhausted mothers slapping at mosquitoes, and the feeble old men bossing everyone about. Tant Minna's wagon may have been bigger than ours, but beneath the heavy canvas shell it looked crowded and stuffy, and as dark as a snake hole. If this was where I'd have to sleep – entangled with my brothers and cousins and our mothers, while Lindiwe and Sipho camped in the open air – I could at least make the most of my solitude while it was still light.

The coppice of thornbushes was just a stone's throw from the edge of the forest. As usual, no one was paying me any notice: the men were too busy marshaling Sipho and Lindiwe into chores, while the women fussed over the blisters on Gert's feet.

Oom Sarel had said that the river was nearby, so I decided to take the opportunity to give my hair a freshwater dousing. I didn't much fancy sharing a bath in the big iron tub with all the other children, where we'd almost certainly be roughly scrubbed by my mother or Tant Minna before being bundled back into the same dirty clothes. *For once,* I thought, *I might impress Ma by turning up freshly washed and combed all on my own.*

The forest was really a sprawling ebony grove. Smooth, slender tree trunks stretched to the sky, forming a quivering canopy of leaves through which sunlight filtered to the forest floor, dappling the ground in greens and golds. Soon enough I came upon the river, which was narrower and shallower than at the point where Gert and I had gone fishing the day before. Kneeling, I cupped my hands in the water and splashed my face and neck. It wasn't as cold as I had hoped it might be; the sun had warmed the riverbed, so it felt more like tepid bathwater. Still, I doused my hair and felt better for it. Something about washing away a week's accumulated grime immediately strengthened my resolve. The world began to look good again.

I decided to continue walking a little farther. There had been rain the previous night, which meant that the ground was strewed with snails. They had come out to gorge themselves on sweet, damp mulch – but the rain had ended suddenly and now they were stranded, like so many tiny shipwrecks. The woods were silent except for the skeletal clattering of leaves through crisp, still air, and the occasional twittering of invisible birds. Farther ahead, a fallen tree blocked my path; its roots had been torn from the ground and towered, glistening and exposed, in the air. I clambered over it and landed with a bump on the other side.

That was when I heard the mewing.

An ebony forest on the edge of beyond is no place for a cat. The next time I heard the cry, I headed in the direction of the noise, scanning the undergrowth for any sign of movement. I must have scared it then, because it fell silent. Just as I had decided to retrace my steps, it mewed again.

This time, I saw it.

The monkey was curled up in the crook of a low branch. Cradling its head in hairless fingers, it moaned softly. From its long tail and tiny, dark face, I could tell it was a vervet. Its downy coat was mostly gray, except for a brilliant white patch on its stomach. Its ears were still too large for its round little head, and it hadn't quite grown into its claws. There was no sign of its mother.

I took another step toward the monkey. Two wide, brown eyes peered down at me defensively, trying to decide if I presented a threat. Something had happened here, I was sure of it. A hyena attack was the most likely explanation – why else would this tiny creature be here all alone, without the protection of mother and pack?

I lowered my gaze and slowly knelt near the base of the tree. I tried to steady my breathing, thinking that by somehow sinking into the background I might avoid scaring the animal away.

We sat like that for several minutes, until I finally dared to steal a look up at the low branch. The monkey had disappeared, and for an instant my heart sank. Then I heard a scrabbling sound immediately behind me, and I swung around, terrified that perhaps the hyenas had returned. Only it wasn't a hyena behind me: it was the little vervet.

Crouched and suspicious, it seemed to waver between curiosity and caution. Slowly, very slowly, I stretched out one hand and rested it, palm up, on the ground between us, clicking my tongue softly in encouragement.

The vervet considered its position, looking from my outstretched hand to my face and back to my hand again, before scuttling toward me. It paused, swaying on bowlegged haunches, eyes wide and alert, bobbing its diminutive head, before craning forward to sniff at my fingers. Its delicate whiskers tickled my palm, and I tried not to flinch. After a while, the monkey stopped, considered me again, and finally drew closer. I froze, pretending that I was a statue, as the vervet proceeded to inspect the contents of my father's coat pockets. First, the left: here a piece from a dry mealie rusk, which it nibbled at apprehensively before greedily licking the whole thing over. When it began to tear into the wet crust, I realized just how ravenous it must have been. Its hunger was even greater than its fear.

The other pocket was empty, but it was so deep that the vervet tumbled headfirst into it before scrambling to right itself. Emboldened, it returned to investigate further – no doubt smelling the traces of the buck meat I had carried home the previous night. When at last the search proved fruitless, the vervet poked its head out of the pocket with a perturbed expression. It was all I could manage not to burst out laughing at its affronted scowl.

"I don't have any food with me," I said, keeping my voice low. "But I could get you something to eat from the *laager*. Would you like that?"

The little vervet only gazed up at me in silent contemplation, gripping the hem of my father's coat with claws so tightly clenched that I couldn't imagine it would ever let go.

THE OX WHIP

"Vermin!"

I cradled the monkey in the pocket of my father's coat while trying not to drop any of the mealie corn that I clutched in one fist. My mother's shrieks pursued us from the wagon into the center of the *laager*.

"Dogs are one thing, my girl, but monkeys are wild animals that grow teeth and have tempers that could kill a boy Hansie's size. I won't have it in the wagon."

"But his mother –"

"His mother left him to the hyenas. If you had an ounce of sense in your head, you'd take him back to where you found him and let the Good Lord's will be done." Ma steeled her jaw, peering down at me like an Old Testament prophet. "There's no use interfering with nature, Corlie Roux."

"I can feed him and keep him warm. He's not dangerous. Look how tiny he is —"

"You can take him back to the forest, or you can give it to Lindiwe to kill for the medicine man."

The *nganga:* he would use my little monkey to bring the rains, or to feed his villagers' poor empty stomachs. As if he, too, knew what my mother was suggesting, the vervet froze in my pocket. I was sure that I could feel his miniature heart drumming through the coat.

"I won't let her give it to the *nganga!*"

"Please yourself — but get rid of it. I don't care how."

Gert followed me to the thornbushes, where I gently tipped the mealie corn into the pocket where my monkey had curled himself into a tiny ball.

"Ma will kill you when she finds out you stole from the mealie sack," said Gert.

"I don't care."

"Can I see it?"

I held the pocket open for my brother to peer inside. The vervet had already devoured most of the corn, greedily cracking each kernel between its teeth. My brother grinned.

"You know, Corlie," he started. "Ma only said you couldn't keep it *in* the wagon."

I looked at him. "What are you talking about?"

"The jockey box is empty. I looked."

The jockey box was a small wooden crate that hung off the back of the wagon. Usually it was used to carry extra supplies, but Tant Minna considered that an invitation to thieves and curious children.

"We could pad it out with straw and take turns feeding it. Ma won't suspect a thing." He had a point: as far as Ma was concerned, neither Gert nor Hansie could do wrong. I was the one who had to be watched. Since Pa's death, it seemed the boys had become that much more precious to her. Because they were precious to me, too, I suppose I forgave her.

"What if he makes a noise?" I asked.

"We'll take him out during the day – you can say that you're going back to the forest to look for him. We'll leave him with lots of food at night."

We both considered the monkey, which was backing out of the pocket so that his spindly tail shot up straight in the air. He began to chatter busily, tugging at the buttons on my father's coat as if they were playthings.

"What will you call him?" asked my brother.

"Monkeys don't have names. He's just that, an *apie*."

"Hello, *apie*. *Hoe gaan dit?*" Gert gently stroked the back of its head, provoking the vervet to twist around and grasp my brother's finger with tiny paws. "*Ag,* you're strong!"

"We mustn't tell Danie or Andries; they'll only tattle to Tant Minna." The creature had begun to coo with pleasure as Gert scratched it gently up and down its back. "The little one isn't out of danger yet."

In the *laager,* each morning began with an impromptu prayer service: one of the women read from the book of Psalms and one of the men led a hymn on a battered banjo. As far as the *Boere* were concerned, worship was never to be neglected, no matter the circumstances. My father had once told me about the Voortrekkers who had been so devoted to their church that they'd taken it along with them into exile. Dutch faithful had dug it up by the foundation, lifted the clapboard frame onto sturdy runners, and hauled the whole thing twelve miles north to build a new Jerusalem farther inland.

After the service that first morning, I took Hansie to join the other kids, who were told to gather firewood and stuff thornbush branches between the spokes of the wagon wheels. The wagons had been chained together to form a ring, and any gaps between the wheels had to be filled to stall potential raiders. I wasn't sure that thornbushes would do much to deter khaki soldiers, but I kept this opinion to myself. Lindiwe and her girls were put in charge of tending the goat that the Van Zyls had brought along: feeding and milking in the mornings, picking its hooves in the evenings, and packing the dung into bricks for fuel. Gert and Sipho were bade to perch on the wagon steps to clean the saddles and harnesses with polish from Oom Cronje's work chest, and I was to sweep the campsite or help Ma with the washing.

These tasks kept us busy until lunchtime, when everyone would gather around for ash-bread or sweet

potatoes roasted in the fire. According to Danie and
Andries, there had been horse meat for a week after
one of the Cronje's mares was found shot in a field
not far from their abandoned farm. While we ate,
Smous Petrus would read aloud from his family Bible,
an enormous book bound in black leather with metal
studs down the spine. After the meal, the men would
spend the heat of the day polishing their rifles and
taking stock of ammunition, while the women shook
out blankets and mended clothing, darning socks
and stitching rag quilts and stopping only to bicker
over whose turn it was to borrow Suzette van der
Westhuizen's crochet needles. The older boys were in
charge of greasing the wagon wheels and grooming
the horses, important tasks that I knew Gert wished
he had been invited to do. At dusk, those boys would
accompany a party of older men down to the river in
search of game; sometimes they would come back
with a wood pigeon or two, but most nights we had to
satisfy ourselves with porridge and biltong, and
perhaps a few sour figs.

More and more, as the days passed, I found myself
counting the hours until the sun would sink below the
fringe of treetops on the distant horizon. I could usually
check on my little monkey after supper, while the rest of
the *laager* remained huddled around the fire, singing
songs and listening to Oom Sarel's tall tales. In just two
weeks, the vervet had grown considerably – its head was
now virtually in proportion to its large ears and wide,

expressive eyes – and I could tell that the time would soon come when it would need to learn to forage for itself. Not just yet, though: the cracking of a tree branch or the whinnying of a horse was still enough to send it scrambling into the folds of my coat, and it continued to suck drops of goats' milk from my fingers with the contentment of a newborn.

One evening, Gert sidled in next to me on the camp-fire bench, his wide eyes telling me of some dreadful change. It had been his turn to feed the vervet, and immediately I sensed that something was wrong.

"He's caught a gecko," whispered my brother, not looking at me but staring straight into the flames as he fiddled with a bit of kindling.

"Where?"

"How do I know? He's taken it into the jockey box. I think he's going to eat it." Gert tossed the stick into the fire, then picked up another. I watched him peel the bark off, strip by strip.

"It's what he's supposed to do," I said at last. "He's becoming wild, that's all. Maybe we should let him go."

"But he's still tiny, Corlie." Gert slid me a nervous look. "Won't you go and see, at least?"

When I opened the lid of the jockey box, I prepared myself for the worst. And yet what I discovered inside took me entirely by surprise.

My little monkey was cradling the flickering green lizard to his chest, cooing softly as the gecko wriggled against the blanket of fur.

When I returned to the campfire and told Gert, he dropped the stick in his hand and faced me squarely. "You're making it up, Corlie."

"No, I'm not – you can go back and see for yourself. He's adopted the lizard – just like we adopted him. Perhaps he's lonely."

"So he's not going to eat it?"

"It didn't look that way to me. We feed him enough as it is."

And so it was that my brother and I found ourselves tending to two small creatures: the orphaned vervet and the gecko it had taken on as its own. Strange as it may sound, we never once saw the lizard try to escape from my *apie*. Instead, it stoically endured the vervet's long bouts of affection – stroking, cradling, and picking off bits of dirt or imaginary fleas – before curling itself up under a clump of grass that we had put in the corner of the jockey box. This lasted for almost a week – and then one morning, Gert discovered that the little gecko had fled.

"A bird might have got it," he whimpered, trailing behind me as I swept the periphery of the *laager*. "It must have left the box when I took *apie* out before breakfast."

As soon as it became clear that the gecko was not going to return, the vervet seemed to sink into a deep gloom. We tried to distract him with trips into the forest and ingenious new toys to keep him entertained: a spinning top, a jar full of buttons, a ball woven out of fabric scraps attached to a leather cord. But nothing seemed to restore its spirits for long. No amount of fussing or food made an ounce of difference – and within just a few days, I could tell that the tiny forlorn creature was beginning to withdraw into itself once again. For the second time in its short life, my monkey grieved.

It was around this time that I caught Smous Petrus hitting Sipho with the ox whip.

I hadn't spoken often to my friend since we'd arrived at the *laager*. The conversations we had shared were limited to practical exchanges – feathering grouse or carrying dried dung bricks from wagon to wagon. I hadn't even had a chance to tell him about Corporal Byrne – and I was ashamed to realize that the soldier was not something I wanted to share with Sipho. The *laager* didn't look kindly on fraternizing with kaffirs. Rumors of African attacks were rife, although how anyone could have picked up such information, I don't know. It was Yvette van der Westhuizen who first whispered to my mother that she'd heard a local commando had been wiped out by an African raid, with only one man managing to escape into the bush where he survived for three days before reaching Standerton.

"The *kaffirs* were after food, that was all," she told Ma as they squatted by the fire, cutting bars of soap. "It was nothing to do with the khakis."

Betsie Gouws had told us that two natives had escorted the Tommies when they came to destroy her neighbor's farm. Once the British soldiers had taken

stock of the contents, they allowed the Africans to loot
the house for whatever food or clothing they wanted. It
was a tactic intended to humiliate the farm owners and
to reward those natives who worked for the British.

"Because there's a war on, they think they can take
what they like from us," said Ma.

It had been her idea to use goats' milk to make the
soap. She and Yvette had acquired oil from Sanna
Wessels and made lye from wood ash; now, at last, the
time had come to break the milky white slab into
chunks to share among the wagons. I watched them,
rolling a bit of soft soap between my palms and wishing
that it smelled less of castor oil.

"If you ask me, we should let the khakis take the
kaffirs back to England with them!" Betsie Gouws
lowered her voice and pointed one finger conspiratori-
ally at my mother. "The English will mix with all sorts,
if it suits them. My Anton says they've even got Indians
fighting for them – what do you think of that? Dressing
up their coolies in a white man's uniform, and calling
themselves a God-fearing people . . ."

"The English are hypocrites," replied my mother.
"They pretend to treat the blacks and coolies as their
equals, but they don't trust them any more than we
do. You won't find a Boer embracing an African with
his left hand and stabbing him in the back with his
right, will you?"

It was all they could do, those older women: bicker
and curse. What did Betsie Gouws know about Indians,

anyway? As far as she was concerned, it had been coolie spells that caused some of our cattle to die the year before last. I had half a mind to tell Ma that if she thought my fairy tales were silly, she should consider all the stupid things Betsie Gouws believed in – but of course I wouldn't dare. I knew that the women moaned like this because they were afraid, frustrated, and exhausted, and all too aware that their hands were tied. If that was what it meant to be a Boer woman, I wanted none of it. I'd stay a girl forever . . . or else I'd disguise myself as a boy and run away to join the men on commando as a girl guerrilla: I'd wear my hair in plaits and make every shot count, and around the campfire each night I'd learn to drink and swear like a man. What honor was there to be found here, squatting over blocks of soap and cursing other people for our problems?

At last I got up and wandered across the campsite to where Lizzie Van Schaeve and Irene Wessels sat making husk dolls. Both were younger than I, all little-girl elbows and knees, and they regarded me with suspicion.

"You can use the silk for hair," I suggested gently. "Comb it together into a plait, and tie it like this – let me show you –"

That was when I heard the screams.

By the time I'd clambered beneath the nearest wagon and wriggled my way toward the other side, Smous Petrus already had Sipho on the ground. Clutching my friend's wrists together in one hand, Smous Petrus was hurling the whip at the backs of Sipho's legs. I felt repulsed and enraged, but also frozen with sickened disbelief – much as I had when Andries once made a show of tearing the legs off a dung beetle. This was worse, however, as I felt Sipho's humiliation with every blow. Each stroke was accompanied by a grunt, an ugly expulsion of air and breath that stank of *dop*. Sipho was struggling to get up, tucking his knees in and pushing his shoulders to the ground – but every time he came close to righting himself, Smous Petrus booted him roughly from behind, sending the boy skidding face-first through the dirt.

"Sneaking off into the bush to meet up with your Zulu friends, eh, *kaffir*?" Smous Petrus's face shone scarlet, and flecks of saliva coated the corners of his mouth. "Getting out of your heads smoking *dagga,* no doubt!"

Sipho said nothing. The pause in the beating was an opportunity for him to catch his breath, and I watched the curve of his spine as it heaved up and down. Sipho would not give Smous Petrus the satisfaction of hearing him weep, and yet from where I crouched I could see that his long, black eyelashes glistened with tears.

I wish that I had done something to help my friend then, but I didn't have time to: all of a sudden Lindiwe appeared out of nowhere, trailing her twin girls in the swirling dust. Both children wailed loudly, their faces streaked with sticky tears, and I realized that they must have been the ones who had alerted her. In an instant,

Lindiwe let go of the girls and lunged at Smous Petrus with fingers spread like claws.

"Let go of my son!" she yelled. Her throat muscles constricted as she hurled herself at him, outlining the taut tendon and sinews of her neck like the roots of a tree. "Let go of him! He has done nothing wrong!"

But Smous Petrus only had to drop the whip and extend one hand to knock her to the ground, and Lindiwe landed with a thud, like a sack of flour. Immediately, Nosipho and Nelisiwe began to scream, tearing at their mother's skirts. This was when I scrambled out from beneath the wagon and found myself confronting the red-faced man.

"Stop!" I shouted. "She's one of ours. The boy, too. They're not yours to beat."

For a fleeting moment Smous Petrus looked as if he might strike out, and I braced myself.

"I'd mind my lip if I were you, *meisie*," he growled, glowering at me with poached eyes. Then, as if he knew what would hurt me more than any physical blow, he added, "If your Pa were here, perhaps I wouldn't have to do his dirty work for him."

He turned on his heel before I could muster a reply, hitching his breeches up around his belly as he strode off into the tea tree bushes.

"Are you all right?" I asked Sipho once Lindiwe had collected herself and bundled the whimpering girls back into the wagon. She must have been able to tell that her son had no wish to weep shamelessly into her

lap. Knowing Sipho, he would be far too humiliated:
like a humbled leopard, he would want to retreat into
the bush to lick his wounds – alone. The backs of his
legs were covered in glistening red stripes, and his lip
had split and swollen, turning an ugly mussel blue.
When Sipho finally brought himself to look at me, I
was shocked to see hate in his eyes.

"It wasn't the Zulu I was following," he hissed
through clenched teeth, cradling his rib cage with thin
arms. "It was the khakis. They know we're here."

A KNIFE FOR GUTTING FISH

They descended on us within the hour, when the sun was still high. Most of the women and children were in the wagons, trying to sleep off the heat of the day. The old men were smoking their pipes; a few had gone to water the horses.

The first shots sounded like snapping branches, and instinctively I looked to the forest, expecting to see dozens of treetops teeter and fall against the milky blue sky. But the trees were still.

Then, a cry: a full-throated call, fearless and shrill. It must have been the voice of a khaki, but at that moment all I could see were rolling clouds of dust barrelling toward us, a thicket of rifles, and the straining heads of horses as they pounded across the plain.

Sipho and I returned to find the *laager* stirring in panic.

"*Laager* up!" shouted Oom Sarel. "Everyone into the center! The horses, too – women and children, behind the barricade!"

Trunks, boxes, water barrels, wagon parts – all were thrown into the center of the *laager* to form a half circle buttressed by piles of gunnysacks. The men scattered to their posts, and the rest of us crowded together: children at the center, women closing the circle at the back. I spied Danie and Andries pressing thorn-tree branches into the hands of other children, bundling stalks twice Hansie's height into my brothers' hands, before Andries rushed to load Pa's gun.

"Give it to me!" cried Gert, tossing his branch aside. "I know how to shoot," he protested, yanking the rifle from Andries.

"You're to stay with the others," said Andries, pushing Gert off. He plunged one hand into a nearby saddlebag, withdrawing a clutch of shells. "There aren't enough guns to go around, and we can't afford to waste bullets."

"Come here, Gert," beckoned Ma. "Keep by me. Corlie, what are you staring at? Get down. Take Hansie."

"We shouldn't have stayed here," whimpered Betsie Gouws. "We should have moved on days ago . . ."

"Don't be ridiculous," snapped my mother. "The Tommies would have found us wherever we went. One of the *kaffirs* probably gave us away." She set her jaw, staring down the frightened woman. "The important thing now is to stay low."

I admired my mother at that moment. It wasn't her

courage that took me by surprise so much as the influence she exerted over the other women. Almost instantly, our little huddle seemed to become resolute, concentrated on survival.

"Everyone knows our men are better shooters," said Ma. "We have nothing to fear from British guns."

I knew this was only partly true. The night before, I'd listened to the men talking around the campfire. "It's not the Tommy guns you should be afraid of," Smous Petrus had warned. "It's their bayonets. Nasty, barbaric thing, a bayonet. In the right hands, one'll slice through a man as easily as if he were a sack of meal." Shooting at the British from a distance was one thing, Smous had explained. As long as we remained an invisible foe, killing khakis was as easy as picking off eggs in a chicken coop. But hand-to-hand combat was a different story altogether.

"Willem Cloete's a crack-shot," mused Betsie Gouws, as if to reassure herself. "He'll pick the Tommies off like tins on a post."

"Marius Botha, too," nodded Lettie Lourens.

I followed the line of her gaze toward Marius, who was unwinding a bandolier from his shoulder to load the rounds into his rifle.

"Someone should run them more ammunition," said Ma, levering open one of the trunks. "Gert, you take these to Oom Willem. Don't linger by the wagon, and come straight back, hear me?"

"Yes, Ma!"

I watched him scurry around the barricade and

across the *laager,* trailing a cartridge belt that he'd slung over one small shoulder. All around us, the men were poised to shoot, waiting for the khakis to come into full view. Almost as soon as my brother returned, landing on the ground next to me with an exhilarated thump, they opened fire.

Startled by the ear-splitting crack of gunshot, a flock of waxbills burst into the air, climbing desperately to reach the safety of the sky. At that moment, frozen with terror, I wished I could have been among them – swimming breathlessly toward the clouds, climbing, climbing – until I was directly overhead and the soldiers below were as small and insignificant as pinpricks. As it was, I could barely make sense of what was happening ten feet in front of me.

"There's heaps of them coming straight for us," shouted Gert in my ear. "Twenty at least, all on horses!"

"Have you seen Sipho?"

"No . . ."

I glanced across the barricade to where Lindiwe was cowering with her daughters. Her lips were moving, forming a stream of soundless words.

"Ma," I said. "Should we pray?"

My mother didn't have time to answer. Behind her, the canvas roof of one of our wagons was suddenly ripped in two by a peppering of shots. A volley of bullets struck the ground not three feet from where we crouched, creating an explosion of dust.

Betsie Gouws screamed and began to tear at her

hair. "We're all going to die!"

"Shut up, Betsie!" My mother grabbed Hansie from me, pressing his flushed face into her skirts, shielding his head, and muffling his wails. She took Gert's head in her free hand, tenderly stroking his white-gold hair for a moment before forcing him to meet her gaze. "You tell Andries to give you your pa's gun," she said. "We're going to fight these monsters. We won't be taken."

I still don't know if she thought my brother might be killed that day. In hindsight, I suppose she was preparing herself for this possibility and making sure that, at the very least, her son would be given the chance of a hero's death.

Without hesitating, Gert rushed to join our cousins. He was still wearing Pa's hat, and from behind, it was difficult to tell him apart from the older boys. By the time he'd made it to the far end of the *laager*, it was almost impossible to see him for all the gun smoke.

"We'll start fires," said my mother as the other women stared dumbly on. "We'll douse rags in oil and launch them at the soldiers. Corlie, you're in charge of the little ones. Ring the edges of the *laager* with your thorn-bush branches: wave them about to create a distraction. The Tommies won't shoot at children."

She spoke to me almost as if I was an equal. Filled with a sudden rush of pride, I leaped to my feet.

"Yes, Ma!" I said, grabbing Lizzie and Irene by the wrists and tearing them from their pleading mothers. Both girls were crying and digging in their heels, so as soon as we were out of reach of the barricade, I spun on them with all the ferocity I could muster.

"Do you want to just sit there like a couple of cows?" I shouted. "Do you?"

"You're horrible!" bawled Irene. "I hate you, Corlie Roux!"

"I don't care," I hollered back. "All I care about is not getting killed by a bunch of filthy khakis. Pick up those branches, and follow me."

To my surprise, they obeyed. We each positioned ourselves between two wagons, balancing on the yoke that hooked up to the axel of the wagon in front, and waved our thorn-tree branches through the gaps — anything to make it harder for the enemy to pick out our shooters. Farther down the line, I saw Lindiwe set herself up in this way with Nosipho and Neliswe. After a while, little Kurt Viljoen joined us, along with his brother Jan, so there were eight of us waving our thorn-tree branches at the advancing army, expelling our terror through wild hoots and hollers.

My mother, meanwhile, was busy setting fires in the center, and the other women began tearing up their aprons and knotting them into bundles to be doused in oil. Out of the corner of my eye, I noticed Tant Minna clamber up on top of one of the wagons to pass ammunition to one of the men. When the man suddenly tumbled from his post just seconds later, she grabbed the rifle from his hand and proceeded to load it herself. I'd never seen my aunt load a gun, let alone fire it. But fire it she did, flattening herself against the wagon canvas and taking aim with all the skill of a practiced hunter. As soon as she shot, she readied her rifle for another round. The fallen man – Jacob van der Westhuizen, who had played his banjo for us every night around the campfire – remained where he had landed, crumpled in a heap on the ground. It took me several moments to realize that he was dead.

The siege can't have gone on for long, but to me it felt as if days passed before the first enemy face appeared between two of the wagons. The soldier was beefy but compact, with mutton-chop whiskers and a fleshy, sunburned nose. Between his teeth he clenched a silver whistle that glinted in the sun. Filling red cheeks as round as apples, he blew with all his might, alerting his comrades to the chink in our defense. Like rats, they poured through the gaps. Lizzie and Irene were the first to flee, screaming, as the soldiers tore the thorn-tree branches from their hands. In an instant the *laager* was swarming with khakis.

Through the mayhem, I caught a glimpse of Sipho lunging at one of the British soldiers from behind, brandishing a knife. It must have been the same knife that he'd taken from my mother's kitchen all those weeks ago, and for an instant I froze in disbelief. Shooting at khakis to defend the *laager* was one thing, but to attack a grown man with a knife used for gutting fish – I couldn't decide whether to be horrified or awed by my friend's bravery.

I didn't see what happened because my brother had

appeared at my side, hair slick with sweat, blue eyes widening in terror.

"There's no more ammunition," gasped Gert. His face was streaked with gun powder. "I fired until I had no more bullets, so Andries gave me some of his. Then Oom Sarel ran out, and Koos Viljoen. Only Oom Willem has any left, and they won't last another round." My brother scanned the chaos around him – the panicked, screaming women, the wailing children cowering beneath their families' wagons, the tired old men struggling against trained soldiers half their age – and his chin began to dimple. "I saw Jacob van der Westhuizen fall from the wagon, Corlie," he said. "Two of the others are dead. Danie was hit in the shoulder – you can see right down to the bone . . ." I watched his shoulders buckle as Pa's rifle slid from his hands to the ground.

"Pick that up," I snapped. "Don't leave Pa's gun in the dirt."

My brother started to lean down to do as I said – but then he froze, his gaze trained on something beyond my shoulder. I turned just in time to see Sipho fly toward Smous Petrus, grasping the glinting blade. The older man was fleeing a pair of soldiers who were calling at him to freeze – "*Staan stil!*" they cried in our language – when Sipho slid beneath his flailing arms, plunging the knife into Petrus's abundant belly. It all happened in an instant: then he was gone. As Smous Petrus fell to the ground, features twisted in rage and anguish at the sight of blood blooming through his sweat-streaked shirt, the soldiers descended on the old man without paying the African boy a second thought.

Had I been the only one to see this, I would never have breathed a word of it. As God is my witness, I would have taken my friend's secret to my grave. But through the commotion, I caught sight of my mother, and I could tell by the expression on her face that she, too, had witnessed the terrible act.

Only then did I realize that our time had run out.

HER HUSBAND'S GUN

We surrendered with a white petticoat tied to a stick. As Oom Willem and Koos Viljoen laid out the bodies of the dead men, Oom Sarel addressed the decimated *laager*. A mounted British soldier remained at his side, gun brandished across his chest. The soldier was such a large man that I felt sorry for his horse. His little black eyes focused on each of us in turn, and I could almost hear him making a mental tally: counting the women and children, adding their numbers to the men's, taking account of the wounded, subtracting the dead. Not twenty yards from where we stood, a group of soldiers was tending to their own casualties. I counted five khaki bodies before my mother cuffed me round the ear and told me to pay them no attention.

"The commandant says that the men will be separated from the women and children," boomed Oom

Sarel. I could tell that he was trying to communicate with as much dignity as he could muster under the circumstances. Behind him, the burned-out shell of our wagon resembled an enormous, blackened rib cage. "Women may take only what they can carry for their families. Everyone must hand in their weapons."

"Where will they take us?" demanded Andries. It was obvious by the way he puffed up his chest and pretended to deepen his voice that he was playing the part of a tough commando. I took Gert's hand and squeezed it tightly.

Oom Sarel turned to the commandant and relayed the question in English.

The commandant straightened, and adjusted his gun.

"Standerton," he said, nodding at the open cart that awaited us. The commandant had peculiarly pointed nostrils, which flared each time he spoke; he wet his lips and the saliva glistened in the sun, demarcating the boundaries of an uncompromising mouth. "From there the women and children will go to Kroonstad." He shot Andries a warning glance. "For their own safety."

"And the men?" asked Oom Sarel.

"The men will become prisoners of war."

Oom Sarel announced that we were to obey the Tommies or else we would be shot. At this, some of the little ones began to whimper. Their mothers muffled their sobs, as tired as they were frightened.

"*Wees sterk, vriende,*" concluded Oom Sarel. *Be strong, friends.*

The men stomped their feet and heckled the British patrol while being chained together at the ankles, until eventually they began to resemble a convulsing, many-limbed insect. My mother told me not to let go of Gert and Hansie – not even for one second. She took Pa's gun from Gert and strode up to the commandant, head held high.

"*Dis my man se geweer*," she said. *This is my husband's gun.* She did not drop it on the ground at the feet of horse and rider, as the others had done, but held it up toward him. The commandant considered my mother, and the rifle. He took the gun and nodded curtly.

"Thank you," he said.

As my mother returned to us, two soldiers appeared with Lindiwe and Sipho in tow. Neliswe and Nosipho trailed behind them, escorted by a third, older soldier, one who looked almost kind.

"We found some blacks trying to escape into the forest," said the one holding Lindiwe, the strange-sounding words emerging through a bristling, gray beard. "The lad's in bad shape, but the woman and her kids are all right."

Sipho was hanging his head so low that the bones on the back of his neck stuck out. I tried willing him to look up, but my friend seemed determined not to meet the gaze of any of us. Lindiwe, on the other hand, fell to her knees the instant she saw my mother, beseeching us with outstretched palms.

"Please, *nooi,* take us with you!" she pleaded. Seeing

their mother in distress, the little girls broke free from the kind-looking soldier and tumbled next to her. Sipho remained where he was, motionless.

My mother opened her mouth to speak, but before she could say anything, Oom Willem's voice rang out loudly over our heads.

"That boy killed one of our men," he said to Oom Sarel. "I saw him stab Smous Petrus – look for a knife with an ivory handle and you'll find Boer blood on it. The hole in that man's stomach was not made by a bullet, any fool will see that."

"No!" Lindiwe dug her fingers into the ground. "He is only a child. He was afraid – we are all afraid. Please, *nooi,* take us with you!"

I looked up at my mother, who had steeled her jaw and was staring intently at the ground between our servants and us. *Please,* I wanted to say. *Do something! You're the bravest one here – tell the commandant that they belong to us.*

"I will not let our women and children travel with a murderer in their midst – so help me, God!" said Oom Willem loudly. "Over my dead body will I allow my daughter onto that cart with a Boer-hating *kaffir.*"

The rest of the *laager* murmured its approval. Even Oom Sarel nodded in agreement.

"The law says that a *kaffir* who murders a white man must be put to death," interjected Koos Viljoen. He turned to the commandant, trying to make the soldier understand. "Even your law says so. The penalty for murder is hanging."

I felt my stomach lurch. I could count the bones on Sipho's neck.

"Gert," I whispered, "I'm going to be sick."

The British soldiers started to realize what had happened, and the commandant began to look uncomfortable. At last, he addressed the soldier who held Sipho.

"The boy shall go with the men," he said to Oom Sarel, to translate. "Charges will be laid. The woman and her daughters will be sent to the African camp at Bethlehem."

As Sipho was led to the wagon where the rest of the men were being settled, Lindiwe let out an anguished howl.

"Please, *nooi!* He is only a child – let him come with me, please! I beg you!"

The two remaining soldiers grabbed her and the weeping girls and pulled them away. Even though his mother continued to scream for him, Sipho did not look up once.

"Do something, Ma," I whispered, tasting the bile rising in my throat. "They can't kill Sipho –"

"*Nooi!*"

Although I could no longer see her behind the wall of soldiers and their horses, the terror in Lindiwe's voice sent a rush of pinpricks up my spine.

"Lindiwe!" I screamed, my eyes stinging with vinegar tears. In that moment, I was overcome with a sensation of being hopelessly suspended in time and space, like a high-wire acrobat anticipating the spring and bounce-back of the safety harness. I heard Lindiwe return my cry – "*Kleinnooi* . . ." – but within a few seconds her wails were drowned out by the soldiers' jeers. By now, Sipho had been lifted onto one of the khaki's horses and was allowing his hands to be tied behind his back. I only had time to call out his name once before Ma's hand came crashing against the side of my head.

"Mind your tongue, or you'll have us all killed!"

My eyes felt so hot I thought they might melt. "Please, Ma," I begged. "Make them promise that they won't hurt Sipho! Please, tell them that Lindiwe must stay with us – for Hansie's sake – tell them . . ." But my words had begun to float away from me, like pieces of driftwood being carried out to sea. "Please, Ma, please . . ." I started to see blotches of color everywhere, the way you do when you close your eyes against a very bright light. Then I heard a thud – the same sound Lindiwe's body had made when Smous Petrus knocked her down – and felt the hot surge of blood gushing between my ears as I hit the ground.

I woke up in the back of a high-sided cart, flanked by my brothers. As soon as he noticed that I was conscious, Gert shuffled closer.

"The *apie*, Corlie," he whispered. "He's still in the jockey box."

"What do you want me to do?" I snapped. My temples pounded; my tongue was so dry that it felt as if it had cleaved to the back of my mouth. Gert shrank back, biting his lip.

It served him right: imagine fretting about a wild animal when Sipho – a person, our friend – might face hanging in a faraway town? And what about Lindiwe, without whom we would never have survived those perilous days on the open platteland? I couldn't allow myself to think of the terrified vervet huddling in its box while battle raged outside, then discovering itself abandoned and alone in the eerie silence that followed – for what was to be done? At times like these, if we didn't harden our hearts against the little things, we would never survive.

There were twelve of us in the cart – all women and children. I noticed Tant Minna standing up at the front, straight as a rod, gripping the side of the wagon with white knuckles.

"Where are Danie and Andries?" I asked.

"With the men," said Ma. She was standing, like the other women, steadying herself against the side of the cart as we rattled over the rocky ground. She eyed me with disdain. "What happened to you, then, eh? Fainting like a princess. What did you think you were doing, drawing attention to yourself like that?"

"You should have said something, Ma. You could have saved them –"

Ma raised her hand. "Don't you speak to me like that, Corlie Roux. All that fuss over an idiot boy with sticky fingers . . ."

In an instant, my grief spun into fury. "You killed him, Ma! You didn't say anything, and now they're going to have him hanged —" I hauled myself to my feet, fighting against the lurching of the wagon. "I hate you!"

She slapped me so hard my head hit the side of the cart, making the others jump. My mother pressed her face toward mine, her breath hot against my skin.

"Don't talk about things you can't understand," she hissed. "You'd have us locked up with a murderer, would you? There's enough evil in our midst as it is, my girl . . ."

She left me slumped in the corner, cupping my head in my palms. The rocking of the wagon had already begun to make me feel queasy.

When we arrived at Standerton soon after, the soldiers herded us like cattle off the cart and into a boxcar that was waiting on a remote strip of rail tracks. It was difficult to see where we were going, and there was no time to gauge our location. Before I knew it, we'd been corralled from the cart into a dark, black box. The only light came from a couple of vents in the roof. When we were all inside, one of the soldiers slammed the door to the boxcar, making the entire thing shake. Moments later, we could hear the engines starting.

I had never been on a train before, and I wished that there might have been a window so I could watch the steam rising from the chimneys. As it was, I could barely make out the shape of my mother and brothers, who had squeezed themselves under one of the air vents. As the train heaved forward, we all stumbled to the back, crushing into one another with shouts of alarm and confusion. It took us a long time to get used to the movement, but after a few minutes everyone became very quiet.

"Are we going to Kroonstad?" Gert asked Ma in a soft voice.

"*Ja.*"

"Why?" There was a long silence. "Why, Ma?"

"Because that's where the Good Lord wants us," replied my mother.

And so it was that we left the Transvaal, and entered the Orange River Colony.

UNDESIRABLES

I t was a burly young khaki who released the boxcar door, hours later. A dazzling square of light cut blindingly into our dark prison, making us wince and shield our eyes from the glare.

"Out!"

We stumbled into the open air like zombies, dropping to the ground and gathering our belongings in a silent daze. Everything seemed to move in slow motion: perhaps because we were dehydrated and sore from the journey, or perhaps it was a tactic employed by our mothers to stall proceedings for as long as possible. They must have known that it would be a long time before we would breathe free air again.

Blinking dumbly at the expanse of veld stretching out before us, we followed the khakis' orders to load a waiting cart with our luggage and to form a line behind it. Then we were made to walk, twenty minutes or so, to the edge of a rocky precipice. In the distance, a winding plume of black smoke rose like a question mark over the horizon. As the cart ground to a halt, I imagined with an intense feeling of sudden dread that we would be made to jump over the edge. I flung my arms around Ma's waist as if she were an anchor, and squeezed my eyes shut. Gert, in turn, did the same thing to me, digging his fingers into my ribs so hard that I gasped.

That was the first time I saw the camp, stretching below us for miles: row upon row of white bell-tents, the lot of them hemmed in by high barbed-wire fencing. Later I would see pictures of the other camps – sprawling prisons at Johannesburg, Bloemfontein, Bethulie, Potchefstroom, and Norvalspont, to name just a few. They all looked the same, more or less: bell-tents and barbed wire as far as the eye could see.

"What is this place?" whispered Tant Minna.

The burly young khaki planted his feet and placed his hands on his hips. Poking out from beneath long khaki shorts, his knees were pink and freckled.

"This is a voluntary refugee camp," he said in our language. "You will be looked after here."

"But we're not refugees," said Lettie Lourens.

The khaki released a bark of laughter. He had a jaw that was straight and pointed like a shovel. "You were found living in the bush," he said. The laughter didn't make his voice sound any friendlier. "You have no homes to return to: that makes you refugees."

"We didn't ask to come here," snapped my mother.

The khaki's eyes narrowed at her. "You only have your husbands to blame for that," he said.

My mother drew herself to her full height and met the khaki's gaze.

"You do this to us because you cannot defeat our husbands on the battlefield," she said. "That makes you cowards."

A collective murmur of agreement rose from the other women. Before the khaki had a chance to respond, Betsie Gouws raised a thin hand.

"When may we have some water?" she asked in a feeble whisper. "The children have had nothing to drink all day."

"There will be water at the camp." The khaki casually indicated the vast scrubland that lay behind us, the miles of railway tracks leading nowhere, and rolled out his thick lower lip, rocking his head heavily from side to side like a boulder teetering over a precipice. "Of course, if you would prefer to dig for water yourselves, you are free to do so." He grinned at my mother. "Otherwise, follow me."

We were led to a checkpoint where a couple of bored-looking soldiers examined us, checking for concealed weapons, before releasing the lock on a metal gate. We passed through two more checkpoints before the last of our group shuffled into the main enclosure.

We were not the only new arrivals. Nearby, a larger group of women and children edged forward in the line for water. We filed in behind them, taking in all that we could of our new surroundings.

The ground under our feet was cracked and dusty, and I wondered how deep the wells must have been to draw enough water for all the inmates. I could not see any trace of a river for miles around. When a breeze built up it blew dust into our eyes and mouths. The tents suffered from the wind, too: they were stained a dirty yellow color from the dust. The people who wandered between them – women and children, mostly, although I did spot a few very old men – stared at us with blank expressions. Some of the women still wore their finest clothes, and it was strange to see them squatting dourly on upturned boxes, stirring soup in their Sunday best. One little child – at first I thought it was a boy, but it turned out to be a girl with sheared hair – tottered up to me, arm outstretched. She was clothed in the scantiest rags, her stomach caved with hunger, her bare feet blistered and filthy, her eyes hollow. In her other arm she supported a tiny infant. As if imitating its sister, the baby clutched at the air with curling, wrinkled fingers, its mouth opening and closing like a fish.

"Please, *meisie,*" the girl said, "Please –" Her mouth was ringed with chapped sores, and a trail of sticky goo dribbled from her nose to the point of her chin.

A woman in a starched uniform squeezed between us,

brushing the child off like a harmless pest. "Ration cards," she bellowed. The woman had arms like ham shanks, thick ankles, and fat, sausage fingers, which she used to hand us square cards listing quantities of food and drink.

3/4 lb mealie meal, to last the week
7 oz coffee (weekly)
14 oz sugar (weekly)
35 oz salt (weekly)
condensed milk
Meat:

☐ *1 lb. meat (twice weekly)*
☐ *1 lb. meat (weekly)*
☐ *none*

"So how much will they give us?" Tant Minna asked Ma.

The woman in the starched uniform grabbed the card from my aunt. "Last name?" she demanded.

"Rossouw."

The woman consulted a clipboard, which hung around her neck by a piece of string. "Your husband is on commando," she noted.

"Yes. We haven't heard from him in almost three months."

The woman scribbled something on the card and handed it back to my aunt. An *X* filled the space next to "none."

"My husband is dead," said Ma as the woman turned

to us. She gathered the three of us around her. "Their father. He died years ago."

As the uniformed woman considered us, the muscles around her nose twitched and quivered as if she was trying to ignore an unwholesome smell.

"One pound a week, for the family," she said, marking Ma's card. "You can collect that tomorrow. There's no more today."

"And the baby? Hansie is only two."

"Can't you read? There's condensed milk for the child." She began to move away from our group. "Queue here to receive your rations," she bawled. "Your ration cards must be completed before you present them at the front . . ."

A bucket of water was passed around while we waited for our rations. Each person was allowed just a few sips from the ladle before it was passed on to the next family in line. In a way, it would have been easier not to drink at all than to have just a couple of drops, which whetted our thirsts without quenching them. With each sip, particles of sand caught meanly in my throat, and I was almost glad to pass the bucket on to Irene Wessels.

We stood and shuffled forward for what seemed like hours before reaching a camp table positioned in front of one of the tents. A man in a khaki uniform took Ma's card and passed it to a boy in the tent. Minutes later, we were presented with a sack of mealie meal and a box containing coffee, salt, and sugar.

My mother began to open the sack to inspect its contents when the man pushed a hand in front of her.

"You can't do that standing in line," he said. "Other people are waiting. Move out of the way."

We did as we were told. When we'd found a quiet spot, Ma ripped open the sack. But almost as soon as we had gathered to peer over her shoulder, Gert and I fell back in horror.

The flour was crawling with maggots. There were so many that the bag seemed to heave with their curling bodies, and even Ma leaped with disgust. When she jumped, half of the flour scattered to the ground.

"No better than floor sweepings!" she gasped, crouching to touch the clumps of grayish matter with hesitant fingers. Before she could stand, a gang of children descended on the maggot-strewn scraps, scraping the ground with desperate fingers for every last grain. With a cry, my mother was knocked to the ground, and I shot to help her.

"Don't touch me, Corlie Roux!"

I recoiled, watching the children disappear between the tents, my eyes stinging.

"They've taken most of our flour," said Gert.

"Quiet, Gert!" snapped Ma.

We were ushered into another line; this one led into a tent that was slightly larger than the others. Gert sneaked ahead to eavesdrop by the entrance, and soon returned with news.

"There are nurses inside," he said. I noticed how the skin on his neck just beneath the bushman arrow had remained perfectly white, like an inverted shadow. Weeks out in the sun with few opportunities to wash meant that the rest of him had long since tanned a ruddy brown.

"It's the surgery," whispered a woman with a face like a peach stone. Her belly was swollen high with child, but looking into those dead eyes I realized that the baby inside her was no better than a parasite, leeching its mother of precious strength. "All new inmates have to be vaccinated."

"My sons have never been vaccinated," huffed Tant Minna, and we were instantly reminded of the fact that they weren't there with us. "They're perfectly healthy boys." Her gruff tone belied the lost look in her eyes, although I knew she would never give the khakis the satisfaction of seeing her grief at being separated from her sons.

"Don't be stupid. You want them to catch measles, or smallpox? Children have died of dysentery, typhoid, and bronchitis this week alone. You take the medicine." The woman grunted at Hansie. "I'd give him a few weeks at best."

"Mind yourself," hissed Ma, lifting Hansie up into her arms and turning her back on the woman. As I watched her smooth his fine curls, I noticed that my mother's hand was trembling.

Some of the other children cried when the doctor jabbed the needle into their bony arms, but I refused to give him such satisfaction. To be fair, the doctor didn't look as if he was enjoying the procedure: all those wailing babies, all those stony-faced mothers, and the relentless heat. But still, he was English: he didn't have to be there. The second he pressed a ball of cotton wool to the spot where the needle had gone in, I snatched it from him and turned on my heel, holding my head high even as my arm began to throb.

Within the hour, both Gert's arm and mine had swollen to double the normal size. The soreness was too much for my brother, who began to gasp and gulp like an infant. I thumped him on his good arm and shot him a look.

"Don't be a baby, Gert. You want the others to think we're soft?"

"Your arm, Corlie –" He pointed. Like his, my arm blushed an angry scarlet, and the lump near my shoulder was turning as hard as a rock.

"You don't see me crying, do you? Or Hansie, for that matter."

We were classed as Undesirables. This meant that we hadn't come to the camp voluntarily and that we had uncles who were still on commando. Families that came of their own accord, and whose men had surrendered – the *hensoppers* – were classed as Refugees. They got extra sugar and real milk and sometimes even the odd sweet potato, and they were put in furnished tents. As we wandered between the rows, we peered into each tent we passed. Some of them housed up to twelve people, while others had only three or four. Nearly every tent had a sick person in it. Some contained empty cots decorated with scrub flowers or bits of black cloth.

Our family – Ma, my brothers, and I – was assigned

to a tent where a family of five was already living. The tent smelled sour, and I had to hold my breath as we were shown to our cots. The woman who lived there was called Agnes Biljon, and although you could see that she was disappointed to have to share the space with new-comers, she did her best to make Ma feel welcome. She told us that she had three children, all girls, aged sixteen, fourteen, and seven. The youngest and the eldest were out collecting rations, while Agnes tended to the middle child, Antjie, who was ill.

Only then did I notice the girl lying against the far side of the tent. Less a girl than a shadow, really: there was so little of her that you would have been forgiven for thinking there was nothing beneath the blankets. She was asleep, and with each breath a tired, wheezing sound escaped through the corners of her mouth. It was hard to say whether or not she was pretty. Her skin was so fine it was almost translucent, the tiny blue veins that traveled to her temples illuminated like branches caught in a flash of lightning. I could tell by her eyebrows that she was a redhead, but much of the hair on her head had fallen out, leaving only the thinnest tangle of flyaway wisps on her bluish scalp.

"It hurts her when I try to comb it," said Agnes, as if she had read my thoughts.

I had expected the white tents to be cool in the midday heat, but ours wasn't: it was suffocating. Perhaps the canvas was too thin; the sun seemed to bore straight through it. The only furniture was a trunk, black with flies, which functioned as a larder. There were no chairs or tables – there wouldn't have been room – and there were just two available cots, without mattresses. Gert and I would have to share one, and Ma and Hansie would take the other.

"We were told a family of five lived here," said Ma, looking around.

"Nandi is our kaffir girl – she's with my daughters right now." Agnes squatted on the ground, making room for Ma to sit on one of the cots. "She was already an orphan, so they allowed her to come with us. They won't provide food for her, though – anything she eats has to come out of our own rations."

"How old is she?"

"Six or seven."

I thought of Sipho, of Lindiwe and her little girls. Where were they now? Had they been vaccinated, given ration cards, and assigned to a bell-tent like ours?

I swallowed, struck by a more pressing question: was Sipho even alive? If the khakis found him guilty of murder, how long would they wait to execute him? I imagined my friend standing before a judge, struggling to understand the soldiers' halting Dutch, and I wondered if anybody would try to defend him. I resolved to pray for him every day, harder than I'd prayed for anyone since Pa was sick. It was all I could do now.

"What's wrong with her?" Ma asked in a voice that was almost gentle, leaning over Antjie. She touched the girl's forehead with a tenderness I'd not seen for anyone other than Gert or Hansie.

"She's starving: nothing will stay down." The other woman's tone, although matter-of-fact, betrayed lost hope. "It's not as if we are eating like kings, but we make do with what we get. The fever is doing this." Agnes dipped a cloth in a bucket of dirty water and wrung it with raw hands. "Because we are Undesirables, we are on the lowest rations. You visit the Merciers' tent across the way and you'll see a healthy family. That's because their father surrendered."

"They should be ashamed," said my mother.

Agnes placed the cloth gently across her daughter's brow and sat back on her haunches. "My husband is still out there, shooting khakis," she said to no one in particular. "This is our punishment. They will make us pay with her life."

While Ma set about heating some milk for Hansie, Gert and I explored the camp. It was then that I noticed the holes that had worn through the soles of both Gert's shoes. He kept tripping over the bit where his toe had rubbed through the leather, and after a while I told him that he might as well take them off. We left them at the perimeter, next to a high fence that shut us off from the brown veld. An hour later, when we passed by on our way back to the tent, the shoes had disappeared.

Gert wanted to use the toilet, so at least there was some mission to our wanderings. After a brief search, we came upon a couple of narrow sheds lined up behind the hospital. Inside was a raised platform with plank seats covered in sacking. My brother peered into a dark hole that had been cut through the plank, and he cupped both hands over his nose and mouth.

"Eugh!"

I looked around for rags. In the outhouse back home, there had been a hook where Lindiwe would hang unwanted scraps of cloth and torn-up newspaper. With a sinking heart, I realized that each and every one of these huts was completely empty. My brother didn't mind – little boys don't – but I dreaded the thought of having to return here later.

When we emerged, a gang of children trundled past us, arms filled with branches and twigs that they must have collected from the edge of the camp where a few pitiful thornbushes grew within the wire fence. Every one of their heads had been shaved, and I wondered how long it would be before we, too, would be subjected to the same indignity.

"Look out, Corlie!"

My brother yanked me aside just in time to avoid being mowed down by a sour-faced khaki hauling a donkey cart. As the contraption rumbled past us, I felt the old queasiness return. Between the restless, pressing bodies of the women who closed in around us, I glimpsed a single white arm hanging from the back of the cart. It was only for an instant; then the crush of bodies squeezed us out of the group, and we found ourselves banished to the fringes.

"How long do we have to stay here, Corlie?" asked
Gert when the sound of clattering wheels had all but
disappeared. He was twisting the bushman arrow back
and forth between black fingers.

"I don't know. Perhaps until the war's over."

"I want to go home. Or back to the *laager*."

"The *laager* doesn't exist anymore."

We had stopped opposite a clapboard building balanced a foot or so above the ground on raised stilts. A
British soldier was sitting on the steps leading up to the
door, and I guessed that this was some kind of daytime
barracks. The Tommy was unwinding his leggings,
revealing skin as white as lambs' flanks underneath. He
had a razor blade clenched between his teeth. As soon
as both legs were bare, he took the razor in one hand and
began scraping – behind the knees, around the ankles.
Here and there, he used the razor to dig into his own
flesh so hard that he drew blood. He grimaced each
time, but he didn't stop.

"What's he doing, Corlie?"

I watched the soldier for a few more minutes, and
then it dawned on me.

"Lice," I said. "He's trying to get rid of the lice." I
smirked at my brother. "Bugs don't care for the
Tommies any more than they care for us Boers," I told
him, trying to make light of it.

When we finally returned to the tent, we learned that
Ma had managed to wash Hansie in one of the slop

buckets. "There's no soap," she said grimly. "And not enough water for both of you." She eyed us up and down before pointing at Gert. "You'll have to stand up in the bucket and Corlie and I will rinse you down," she said. "Agnes says that someone stole her last blanket, so you'll have to dry in the open air. At least it's still warm – goodness knows what happens in winter."

She had changed out of her heavy gingham dress and stood in under-bodice and bloomers. I watched her bend to pick up the bucket and was struck by how small she looked without her usual armor of petticoats and a stiff, high-necked collar. Indeed, my mother's body might as well have belonged to a complete stranger, reflecting surprisingly little of her severe disposition. Her hairless arms were lightly tanned, the smooth undersides vulnerable and white, and the telltale creases above her upper lip remained the only imperfections on a still youthful face. I knew the stories of two tiny scars that I glimpsed only very rarely, when she took to the barrel tub to wash after Gert and I were in bed: a white, raised *V* on the inside of her left armpit where a pet parakeet had scratched her as a girl, and a line of pockmarks high up on her right thigh where she had fallen on some gravel outside the church after her wedding to my father. These marks were embarrassing to me, though I couldn't say exactly why. The well-defined muscles of her calves, shoulders, and abdomen, the folds of skin behind her knees, and the strands of hair that wouldn't be tamed into a bun but formed little floating halos above her ears – all seemed hopelessly foreign and apart from me.

I had never felt this way about my father. There was no mystery hidden in the hatch marks of the crinkled, leathery skin on the backs of his hands or within the tangle of dark hairs that dovetailed down his shins. The hammerhead toe that was so curled it couldn't be forced flat, the candle-taper fingers, and honest, square finger-nails were as familiar to me as my own. I had memo-rized them long ago, and I searched daily for their echoes in my own feet and hands. Sometimes I saw them; mostly I didn't.

Halfway through that first night, I woke up in a pool of wetness and instantly felt a chill of fear run through me: what would Ma say when she found out? Bed-wetting was excusable from a child Hansie's age, but there was no defending a twelve-year-old girl who couldn't wake up in time to relieve herself.

Outside, the first gray light shimmered. Further inspection of my cot revealed that I'd not wet myself, after all. The water was dew: moisture that had drained in off the tent, and Gert and I were both soaked through.

That same morning, Antjie was transferred to the hospital.

HEROD'S WORK

The doctors came for her just as Ma was taking the scissors to Gert's hair. My mother was so busy trying to hold back her welling tears she didn't even have breath to curse the British nurse as Antjie was wrapped in a musty-smelling blanket and levered onto a stretcher and carried out of the tent. When they had gone – the doctors and Antjie and Agnes, who was supported by her two other daughters and Nandi – Ma snipped the last of the golden tendrils that curled behind Gert's ears and collected the strands into a bundle.

"So much hair, *boytjie . . .*" she said wistfully. I wondered if she was going to tie his hair with a ribbon and treasure it as a keepsake, the way people did in olden times.

My brother rubbed his head with both hands and grinned.

"It feels lighter," he said.

I told him that he looked like a drongo chick, and Ma cuffed me upside the head.

"It's your turn next, my girl."

Agnes had told us that there was no point waiting for the lice to come before cutting our hair; she said it made it easier to pick them out if you worked off a shaved scalp. As much as it pained Ma to shear her sons like a couple of gormless lambs, she seemed to have little difficulty tearing through my mousy locks. Gripping a clutch of hair in one hand, she managed the scissors like they were a scythe slicing through mealie shoots.

It's just hair, I thought. And yet, the way she pulled at it made me think she hated my sandy-brown curls. Lindiwe had once observed that my hair looked red when the sun caught it, the color of tea – something that I'd taken as a compliment. But when I proudly reported this to Ma, my mother had flown into an instant rage. Lindiwe had no right to say such things, she'd said. And I was a vain and stupid girl to think my hair was anything special. She told me she'd sooner see it all cut off than tolerate such nonsense about having a redhead in the family.

She couldn't have known then that one day she'd get her wish.

There was no mirror in the tent to inspect the results. All I could do was feel my head with astonished fingers and look to Gert for affirmation.

"You look funny."

"Not as funny as you," I snapped.

We hung about the tent until midday, when Agnes returned with her two daughters and Nandi. The smallest one seemed to have taken a liking to Gert, so the two of them puttered about outside while Ma and I brewed some bush tea for Agnes and the older girl. Her name was Marieta, and I thought her quite beautiful: raven-haired, with eyes the color of grass after a storm, porcelain skin, and a queen's stately bearing. She wore a white pinafore over a robin's-egg blue dress, and somehow she managed never to look as dusty or rumpled as the rest of us. She rarely spoke, and when she did, it was in such a low voice that I wondered what must be going through her head. I longed to be so composed, so dignified, to measure my words so carefully, to speak with such grace. Marieta was her mother's rock. She supported Agnes with hands that were at once gentle and strong, and I struggled to imagine ever mustering the courage to do the same for Ma.

"The nurses were going to classify her as an idiot," Agnes was saying. Her nose was red and her voice trembled, but her eyes were cold with fury. "Just because they couldn't understand her words. Antjie was delirious; of course she wasn't making sense. But to suggest that she isn't mentally fit –"

"They know she is fit, Ma," soothed Marieta. "We told them she is. They were only trying to make excuses."

"Cruel excuses! My Antjie used to write poetry; she could paint like a dream –"

"When will she be released?" asked my mother.

"They wouldn't say. They asked if we wanted her to be photographed, in case she dies . . ."

Ma struggled to conceal her surprise. "Photographed?"

"As a memento. A keepsake. For her father."

The tea was brewed; there were only three cups. I wandered out into the sunshine, taking a moment to let my eyes adjust to the glare. A bowlegged man was staggering down the gangway outside our tent, a long laneway that cut all the way from one end of the camp to the other. Some of the women had named it Steyn Street, after the Free State president. With one hand the bowlegged man hauled a stuffed gunnysack along the path; the other brandished a pair of ladies' bloomers at passersby.

"That's Errol Joubert," said a woman sitting outside the tent opposite ours. She smiled up at me from beneath her cotton bonnet, running a tip of thread across her tongue before poking it through the eye of a sewing needle. "A right *skollie,* if ever there was one. Never trust a man with eyes like a shore bug, my girl. You'll see him trying to sell the darkness of Egypt next – anything for a twist of tobacco or a few drops of *dop.*"

"Is he a *hensopper?*" I asked in a low voice.

The woman's smile spread across her freckled face. I guessed that she was younger than my mother, but older than Marieta.

"He'll tell you that he fought alongside Theron himself just three weeks ago," she said. "The truth is anyone's guess."

"I can't picture him with Danie Theron." Everyone knew that Lord Roberts had described the heroic young scout as "the chief thorn in the side of the British."

"A few days ago, I'll bet you couldn't picture a place like this," she replied.

"We knew there were camps," I told her, not to be taken for a fool. "We just didn't know it would be . . ."

"Hell?" The woman set her sewing aside and beckoned me forward. "Are you the girl with the little brothers?" I nodded. "You mind your Ma takes care of the baby," she said. "Do you have milk?"

"A bit."

"Good." She reached into a tin obscured by the folds of her skirt and withdrew a corner of bread. Her hands were long and thin. "Here, take this." She waved it at me as I stared incredulously at the first piece of solid food I'd seen since arriving at the camp. "Go on. It's real. A bit stale, I'll admit. My sister died last week, but I'm still collecting her rations. Get your brother to bring me fresh kindling in a day or so, and I'll see to it that you don't starve." The smile faded as I reached out for the bread. "They took her to hospital this morning, is that right? The Biljon girl?"

"That's right."

"God have mercy."

Her name was Annie Steenkamp. The next day, after bringing her a bundle of kindling scraps we'd collected from the periphery, reaching our skinny arms through the barbed wire to grab at twigs and bracken just beyond our prison, she gave us an apple that she had found among the slops behind the officers' mess.

An apple!

It was small and shriveled, but Gert and I couldn't have been more excited. Neither of us had tasted fruit for weeks. We took it off to a quiet place behind the toilet sheds, where I tore off a few pieces with my teeth and passed them to my brother. It was the nicest thing we'd eaten since arriving at the camp.

Over the next few days, I got to know some of the other women in our block. I made a point of targeting one tent per row: that way, they were less likely to catch wind that I was running errands for all of them. Heila Du Preez, Lynette Bekker, Sonja Erasmus – they were the most generous with their handouts. I tried to choose mothers whose children had died, as they were more likely to take pity and now had fewer mouths to feed. By the second week, I was taking food from six different women, none of whom knew that I was being fed by the others.

Maintaining that deception was just about my only pastime. Most people at the camp simply sat about waiting for the war to end. Time moved more slowly here than it did back home. It was measured differently, too. On the farm, the cock's crow and the height of the sun had told us when it was time to rise, to rest, and to eat; here, our lives were regimented by the curfew bell and the interminable ticking of the hospital clock.

It didn't take long for me and Gert to grow numb with boredom.

"Tell me a story," he would say. But after a few days of telling tales about Ntombazi, my brother grew restless and whined about being bored by the exploits of the African queen who had her enemies buried alive within the high palace walls.

So I devised a fresh tale in which all of the characters were animals. My brother and I had seen all we needed to see of human suffering, and it was the wild beasts of the veld that helped us escape into our memories. We still talked about the vervet, and wondered what had become of him after the *laager* was abandoned.

"There once was a little dikkop," I began, "that had spotted wings and knobbly knees, and a tiny voice that squeaked. He lived alone in a nest built into a *koppie* overlooking a huge lake, and he used to dream of going down to the water to drink and spy for fish. But the lake was guarded by great, belching hippos, who everyone knows are by far the most dangerous animals in all of Africa."

I paused here, waiting for Gert to urge me to continue. By this point, one or two other children had stopped to listen, idly staring on with wide eyes and slack jaws.

"Even more troubling to the little dikkop were the rhinos, who would bellow and rear their horns at the slightest nuisance. You might think that the dikkop would simply fly over their heads, but he was too afraid – and when a dikkop is fearful, it can't fly. The only thing it can do is run, but to do this it must keep its head lowered, and this causes it to lose any sense of direction and makes the animal become even more panicked. The little dikkop knew this, and so he never dared to venture off of his *koppie*.

"One day, a klipspringer came up the *koppie*, looking for something to eat. He greeted the dikkop, who at first was afraid of this four-legged creature with long, twisting horns. But the klipspringer was friendly, and said, 'You and I aren't so different, little dikkop: I can leap almost as high as you can fly. That makes us virtually brothers.'

"The dikkop considered this before saying, 'But you don't need to drink to survive: everyone knows that you get all the water you need from the leaves you eat. I, on the other hand, am thirsty but too frightened to go down to the water alone.'

"The klipspringer considered the stretch of land between the *koppie* and the lake, and he noticed the rhinos and the hippos sunning themselves on the riverbank.

"'I'll take you to the water,' he said at last. 'Hop onto my back, and hold on tight.'

"The dikkop did as he was told, and at once they were off, bounding left and right, so that the rhinos – who have a sharp sense of smell but very poor eyesight – would not see them. At last they reached the riverbank, and the dikkop slid to the ground.

"'There you are,' said the klipspringer.

"'But what about the hippos?'

"'Even the hippos can use a bit of help from time to time. They won't mind you sitting on their backs as they float through the water as long as you make sure to snap up any mosquitoes that start to bother them. That is the secret: know your enemy. Then freedom will be yours.'

"'Is that why you helped me?' asked the dikkop, suddenly suspicious. 'Because you wanted something in return?'

"The klipspringer laughed. 'Of course not, you silly dikkop,' he said. 'I helped you because you are my brother.' And he bounded off into the sunset."

The story failed to satisfy Gert. "That's stupid," he said at the end. "The little dikkop should have pulled himself together and flown down to the water on his own. If he was so afraid, he deserved to die of thirst on the *koppie*." The other children murmured their agreement, listlessly nodding heads too large for their emaciated bodies. "And anyway," continued Gert. "No klipspringer would help a silly bird just for the sake of it. Life isn't like that."

I scowled at him. "Lindiwe and Sipho helped us," I said. "And they didn't get anything in return." I cocked my chin at the other children, daring them to contradict me. "Anyway, you're all no better than the little dikkop yourselves. I haven't seen anyone here try to escape – and do you know why? Because you're all too afraid."

At this, Gert bit his lip and stared down at the ground. After a moment, he cast his gaze up, out past the barbed-wire fences and sentry posts to where the veld stretched toward the horizon.

"General De la Rey's out there," he said. "Ma said that him and Botha are nearby, planning to help us escape. They're just biding their time."

The Lion of the West Transvaal. He of the long beard and formidable brow, De la Rey had attained legendary status in our camp. Our mothers told us that he had twelve children of his own and looked after six more who had been orphaned – that he would sacrifice everything for them, and for us.

One of the younger boys in the group turned to me. "It's true," he said through gap teeth. "My ma says De la Rey's like Moses when he led the Children of Israel through the wilderness. Not even Pharaoh's army could catch them." He turned to the others. "He knows we're here. The khakis *want* him to know: that's the whole point. If the commandos hear that little children have died in the camp, they'll surrender." He flinched as Gert shot him a look. "Only De la Rey won't let them – just last week I heard some of the khakis saying there had been gunfire near the river basin."

"He hasn't given up," said Gert, looking smug. "He's out there. He'll come."

I smacked him sharply. "And what does that make us? Nice juicy bait, that's what!" I turned to the other children. Immediately the other boy lowered his eyes, monkey mouth clamping shut. "My ma says that De la Rey releases any British soldiers he captures," I told them. "That's weakness, that is. He should have them shot."

We all considered the gaps in the wire fence that framed the great expanse of empty land, listening for the distant crump of shellfire. My brother stuck his thumb in his mouth, and sucked hard. It was something he had started to do lately, reverting to babyish habits, and it made my blood boil. Before I could snap at him to stop, Gert turned away and wandered slowly back to our tent.

Soon, even death became mundane. I don't think that my brother really understood it at first, when he heard women talking about the children they'd lost. To my brother, "lost" was something that happened to children in fairy tales. It was hard to believe that healthy boys like him – and younger ones, too – could die before they'd even had a chance to fight the Tommies. Every few days we would watch a family place a new tiny bundle outside a tent, and before long we wouldn't even think of the body swaddled inside. The lucky ones were put in soap boxes, two to a coffin.

My brothers and I didn't join the crowds of children that chased after the death cart, and we didn't keep a tally of invalids and deaths the way some of the others did. We all watched our mothers handle their suffering in different ways. Some would weep shamelessly, others would rage, some went mute, and a few – Ma was one of these – seemed to take a defiant pride in their pre-dicament. In every case, numbness would finally take over. It floated in constantly from across the veld and settled in as a blanket over the camp, leaving its residue on the dusty ground beneath our feet, only to be tracked into the tents, where it infected our hair and clothes and the very air we breathed. These days, for every refugee that died, there were a dozen more waiting to be let into the camp. One morning, Gert told me that he had seen the superintendent sitting at his desk with his head in his hands just moments after the arrival of a fresh group of inmates who had been sent from the camp at Bethulie, which was now full. Because there were no more tents for them even here, the women and children had to sleep out in the open veld.

By the time word arrived that Antjie Biljon had finally passed away in hospital, none of us was terribly surprised. It was as if her death had been hanging in the air for days before it happened, by which time we'd already learned to live with her mother's muffled sobbing and her little sister's wide, blank stare that followed us around the tent like a shadow.

The strangest thing about being surrounded by so much suffering, so many invalids and cadavers and walking ghosts, was that my memories of Pa became more vivid by the day. I saw him in the bread queues and loitering outside the hospital; I saw him tending our small fire and rocking Hansie to sleep with all the flies buzzing around. Pa was real. Everything else was just a dream: a horrible dream from which I would wake to find myself at his side, squatting on our front porch, peeling a mango, and counting fireflies late into the night.

Ma and Agnes caught the Biljon's servant girl stealing from the mealie bucket and locked her in a wooden trunk for three hours as a punishment. The trunk was about three feet tall, four feet long, and two feet wide: large enough to hold a six-year-old girl, though still too small for her to turn around. It made me remember my *apie* in the jockey box – a thought that filled me with sudden sadness. Agnes, Marieta, and Ma pretended not to hear Nandi's screams for the first half hour or so, and eventually she went quiet. I knew that she wouldn't suffocate, as there were a few gaps where the wood had splintered, but still I planted myself nearby so that I could whisper reassurances to her when the others weren't looking. It seemed to me that being locked in the trunk must have felt like being buried alive.

Ma called her a snake in the grass, a cockroach that deserved to be stamped on. She told me and Gert that we were to keep saying our prayers every night if we didn't want to hear the same voice of temptation that had led Nandi to commit such a wicked act; she said the devil would try to whisper to us at night through the wall of our tent, but that he would be frightened away if we prayed hard enough. It had been Ma's idea to lock Nandi in the trunk as a punishment and as a lesson to the rest of us. Marieta had been the only one to protest, saying that the child couldn't help it: all Africans were alike, more animal than human, and an animal's instinct is to scavenge for food wherever it can.

"Sipho's not an animal," I'd interjected. I didn't like to disagree with Marieta, but I couldn't help it. "Besides, Gert and I scavenged when we were out on the veld – Ma told us to collect groundnuts. Does that make us animals, too?"

Marieta had looked at me uncomfortably. "That's different" was all she said.

Nandi's timing couldn't have been worse: only the day before, three more children in nearby tent rows had died – two in the same family, a couple of tents from ours – and now everyone's nerves were on edge. The three had been laid out together, each with a tiny white flower, for people to come and pay their respects and for photographs to be taken for the absent fathers.

"Murdered innocents," people said in hushed tones. "The British are doing Herod's work."

None of the children had been treated in the medical tent because most people believed that children only went there to die. And since no visitors were allowed in the hospital, many of the women dreaded the thought of their little ones being taken away lest they never be seen again. Once I saw a woman prop up the half-dead body of her infant in a chair, and another time I caught sight of a mother leading a toddler on a walk around the camp while the older sibling supported the suffering child from behind – all to make it look as though the tiny ones were perfectly healthy, to avoid arousing suspicion from the matrons. Moving them kept the blowflies off their bodies and prevented the red ants from crawling into their eyes.

Our mothers used old remedies to ease the suffering of family members: swaddling an inflamed chest in dung and animal skins, treating open wounds with licorice plant leaves, and sealing the tent to sweat out a fever. It was well-known that the doctors didn't think much of our remedies; but then, we didn't think much of theirs. The English nurses were under-trained and overworked, and one of the doctors was a notorious drunkard.

Most of the time, it was impossible to tell if a child was suffering from malaria or typhoid or blackwater fever. Victims of these diseases all started to look the same after a while: emaciated bodies stretched out like faded flowers scattered on a bed, eyes hollow, skin clammy. A rash indicated measles or smallpox; coughing was usually bronchitis. Diarrhea was a sign of flux, though it was common enough even among the relatively healthy.

Gert twice returned to our tent with blood smeared across his upper lip, but Ma put that down to a burst vessel brought on by the dry air. In a place where several people died every week, no one paid much attention to nosebleeds – and so Gert continued to be sent out to collect kindling with the other children until the day he fainted. Even then, we assumed it was only the heat. Ma didn't believe in headaches, so we'd not worried when he'd said that morning that his eyes were sore.

In the end, it was Marieta who first noticed the cluster of tiny red spots on his chest.

AN EGG

After two days, Gert started refusing food.

Ma said that aloes and egg whites were the best cure for typhoid, but neither was to be found in the camp. I spent an entire day wandering along the tall wire fence, gazing out at hardy clusters of spiky green aloe plants fringing the hills just a hundred yards from where I walked. Women had begged the British soldiers to let them go out to collect the plants to treat their ailing children, but permission was never granted. As for eggs, they were considered too fragile to be worth shipping to the camps. Heila Du Preez had once lured a few hens in through a hole in the fence, but these birds — apparently mangy, poor layers, anyway — had died off just before we'd arrived.

I found Heila scrubbing her nephew's breeches over a barrel of gray water. The boy, Frikkie, squatted nearby.

A few days earlier, he had been bitten by a brown button spider. We knew it must have been a brown button spider because a black one would have killed him in no time at all. The bite site was white, encircled by an ugly red rash, and today Frikkie was dabbing at it with a wet cloth.

"You need aloe for that," I said.

Frikkie looked up at me, squinting into the sun.

"What do you think *this* is?" he retorted. His aunt snapped the breeches at him.

"Mind your tongue, Frik!"

I knelt at Heila's side and lowered my voice.

"Where did you find it, Heila?" I asked. "If you tell me, I promise I won't say a word."

Heila resumed her scrubbing, avoiding my eye.

"Please, Heila," I whispered. "It's for Gert. Ma thinks it could be typhoid."

She looked up at me, and I saw anger vanish from her gaze only to be replaced with something new. Fear.

"How does she know?"

"He has the rash. At first we thought it might be dengue fever, but Lettie Lourens thinks his nosebleeds might have been a sign." I lowered my eyes, praying that she might take pity. "Ma says we need aloe and egg whites for a poultice."

"The hens are dead."

I hesitated, taken aback by the edge in her voice. After a moment, Heila Du Preez rose and disappeared into the tent. She returned with a skin flask, which she passed to me. Tilting it between my hands, I felt a dribble of fluid inside.

"The khakis thought it was only water."

I almost extended my arms to embrace her, but something about the way she held herself stopped me.

"Thank you, Heila," I said. "Thank you, thank you . . ." I turned to go back to our tent.

"Corlie Roux."

I stopped and turned, terrified that she was going to make an impossible demand. "I'll bring more kindling tonight; I promise," I blurted. "And some mealie meal, too. Ma is so worried about Gert she's hardly eating –"

"See Lynette Bekker about the eggs," she whispered, not looking at me as she returned to her scrubbing. "The Tommies keep chickens near their barracks."

Lynette Bekker spent one day each week working in the barracks laundry, services for which she was paid in mealie corn. Thanking Heila a second time, I hurried on.

As I made my way between the rows of tents, I said a silent prayer – not so much for my brother as for myself. *Please, God,* I thought, *don't take Gertie. You already took my Pa, and Sipho, and my little* apie. *You can't take my brother, too.*

When I had left the tent that morning, my brother's eyes were rolled back in his head as he slept. Agnes helped Ma to change him out of his sweat-drenched breeches and into a clean petticoat that had once belonged to Antjie. I hadn't wanted him to wear anything that had belonged to someone who was now dead, but it wasn't the time for me to protest. Gert had been moaning and mumbling to himself all through the night, and none of us had slept well.

That morning I had crept close to my brother's side and whispered in his ear.

"Pull yourself together," I had said. "There will be a lot of work for us to do when the war ends, and you'll need all your strength. The first thing we'll do is get the farm up and running – that's what Pa would want. The khakis can't keep us here forever, Gertie . . ."

Ma had pushed me aside before I had a chance to say anything else – before I had a chance to tell my brother that I loved him, that he was my only friend in all the world besides Sipho, that I couldn't bear to think of going back to our farm without him – and in that instant, I realized that she would have preferred me to be lying in that bed.

"Are you trying to smother him?" she had snapped.

Yes, it was true: my mother would rather I died in his place.

Ma refused to admit that he was delirious. "He's been having bad dreams," she said to our neighbors, to explain why we all looked even more exhausted than usual. "Night terrors, that's all."

But I knew there was more to it than that, and – judging by the way she watched over him – I was pretty certain that she did, too.

"I thought the immunizations were supposed to keep our children healthy," I'd heard her mutter to Agnes in the early hours of morning. "Otherwise, what are they good for?"

"Khaki propaganda," she replied.

I was jolted from the memory by the sounds of a scuffle behind one of the tents. Poking my head into a narrow passageway, I watched aghast as two women tore at each other like a couple of enraged cats. On the ground lay an overturned tin of condensed milk, the contents of which had already begun to seep into the yellow ground.

"Thief! Thief!" cried several other women who had also sought out the source of the noise. The two scrappers – a burly, red-faced *vrouw* with hands like spades, and a wiry younger woman whose hair had become unpinned in the fray – tumbled to the ground.

Without stopping to think, I made a dash for the tin. If I could only save a few drops of milk, it would keep Hansie fed for another day and we could give the rest of our water to Gert –

"Another one!"

A hand hit me roughly on the side of my head, and I hit the ground with a yelp.

"Scavenger! Thief!"

I was hauled to my feet and shoved to one side as a crowd of children descended upon the now empty can. When I looked up, I recognized Sonja Erasmus – one of the women from whom I had taken regular hand-outs over recent weeks. She glowered at me with eyes like raisins planted in a swollen, doughy face.

"Snatch and grab, will you? While the women behave like children, the children behave like animals!" She smacked me again, and despite myself my eyes smarted. "You're nothing better than a stray, Corlie Roux. We may have fed you our scraps, but you were never welcome in our tents. Brazen greed! That's the thanks we get for taking pity on a mongrel, for turning a blind eye to your mother's sins . . ."

I wriggled away from her and ran as fast as my feet would carry me, not stopping until I reached the Bekkers.'

"Ma!" I cried, holding out Heila's flask as I burst into our tent. "Aloe water, Ma! And Lynette Bekker promised that she would try to steal us an egg tomorrow –"

Inside, the air hung thick and heavy. For almost two days, Ma had kept the tent sealed so that Gertie could sweat out the fever. Despite our best efforts, dozens of flies swarmed about the bed. Hansie knelt next to my brother, swatting at the flies whenever they tried to settle on him.

"An egg, Ma," I repeated. "And you know what that means: we can put the whites in a poultice and we can eat the yolk . . ."

My mother was standing in the middle of the tent, staring at the ground. Agnes and her daughters were not there. On my way, I had passed Nandi carrying the day's water ration back to the tent. The tiny girl had gripped the bucket's rope handle with chafed fingers, concentrating hard so as not to spill a single precious drop as she shuffled down Steyn Street. Had it been any other day I would have stopped to help – but in my excitement about the egg I'd rushed straight past her.

My mother didn't appear to have heard me. She remained where she was, still as a tree trunk, both arms limp at her sides; a strange, soft, choking noise emanated from her lips. I rushed closer, pressing the flask toward her.

"There's just enough here –"

"Look at him, Corlie Roux," said my mother. Her voice sounded the way it always did when she was about to rant – full of spite and simmering rage – and instinctively I drew back. But Ma remained exactly as she was, staring at the floor with blank eyes.

I turned toward the bed. Gertie's head had tipped to one side, away from me, and I could tell that his mouth was slightly open. Patches of yellow hair had started to grow in place of his beautiful golden forelock, and a few fine wisps still curled about his ears. The white petticoat was wrinkled and sticky with sweat, but my brother looked peaceful. I edged nearer.

"Gertie?" I whispered.

The bushman arrow still hung from the leather cord around his neck. I suddenly noticed how bright it seemed against my brother's gray skin.

That was when I realized he was dead.

"He hasn't moved for two hours," said Ma. Her voice sounded as if it belonged to someone else. "I've been waiting for him to move. He won't move."

I dropped to the ground next to my brother, and extended one hand to touch his cheek.

"Gertie –"

"Don't touch him!" Ma lunged at me, fingers digging like daggers into my arms as she hurled me across the tent.

I cried out as I hit the ground, but when I went to raise myself, the wind had already been knocked from my lungs, and I gasped for air.

"Don't come anywhere near him!" shrieked my mother. Behind her, Hansie sat staring. His face crumpled, breaking out in angry, red blotches as tears began streaming down his cheeks.

I cowered in the corner where I had landed, desperately trying to form words.

"He's my brother," I wheezed.

"Yours! Yours!" Ma's clenched hand swept over the table, sending cups, plates, and a broken lantern across the floor. Hansie screamed and began pummeling the bed with balled fists. "Selfish, insolent girl! Wicked, evil, godless girl!" Before I could slide out of her reach, she grabbed me by one arm and hauled me out of the tent. Behind us, Hansie's howls grew louder.

"I didn't ask for you," she growled. "If I could have that boy back and you cold in the ground, I would. As God is my witness, I wish you had never been born, Coraline Roux!"

I could sense that we were being watched, but at that

moment, my full attention was focused on my mother. Grief had distorted her handsome face so that it seemed ugly. She grabbed the flask of aloe water and flung it at me.

"Take your blasted aloe," she shrieked. "The Devil take you!"

"I will!" I shouted back. "I'll leave, and then you'll only have Hansie, the way you've always wanted!"

"Leave?" My mother dissolved into poisonous laughter. "Where will you go in this godforsaken place?"

"I'll look after myself." And then, because I couldn't stop myself, I added, "I could have looked after Gert, too."

If she'd had the chance then, I think my mother would have tried to kill me. She certainly looked as if she wanted to: every fiber in her seemed geared to wring my neck. But then a British soldier appeared – I recognized him as the one Gert and I had watched picking lice from his legs on the barracks steps – and instantly the light in Ma's eyes seemed to change.

"Here," she called, pointing at me. "Take this girl!"

The soldier looked down at me, his expression a mixture of confusion and pity.

"Take her!" repeated my mother. If it weren't for her rage, I might have thought that she was pleading with him. "Go on, you fool – she's one of yours!"

THE DARKNESS OF EGYPT

Those were the words that haunted me as I lay curled beneath the khaki barracks at the edge of the camp. Winter was just around the corner, and the dry, crisp days were starting to give way to cold nights. Just the other morning, Gert had woken to discover frost flowers forming in the clay outside our tent. What I wouldn't give for it to be October again, when steaming sunshine and warm thundershowers wrapped us in the earthy smells of the veld. It was still only April, and yet my father's coat offered limited protection from the chill.

I fell in and out of sleep, dreaming that my brother was there beside me. I heard my mother's words, and the words of Sonja Erasmus – she had called me a mongrel, but why? Then, my brother's voice. "Tell me a story, Corlie," he pleaded. My mind teemed with imaginary characters – Ntombazi, the little dikkop that was too frightened to fly, the fisherman's son who discovered a monster on the shore – but before long, their stories began to blur so that I didn't know where to begin. I saw my brother's round, white face watching me as I struggled to find the words. I noticed the petulant curl of his mouth, and as he turned away I heard Ma's voice again. Only, the thing that spoke wasn't my mother, but a magnificent lioness. The creature's thick, muscular neck and powerful claws were stained red, and for a terrible instant I glimpsed my own reflection in its gleaming yellow eyes. The next thing I knew, the lioness reared up and let out a glorious roar.

Later, as I fell into a deeper sleep toward the early hours of the morning, I dreamed that I was walking through a forest. Black trees formed a thicketed ceiling beneath the inky sky, and the darkness had the same touch, the same scent as breathing earth: like the sweet soil that had turned and churned – softly, soundlessly – under my father's plow. The sounds of leaves twisting on their branches only accentuated the silence. Between the swaying canopy, I could make out distant constellations, like glistening nails pinned to the sky.

Suddenly, a flash of light tore the sky in half, peeling back the layers of darkness to expose a blinding streak of white fire. I barely had time to cover my eyes before a luminous ball of flames swept across the treetops, trailing a sparkling ribbon of debris in its wake. In a single second, everything was illuminated by a silver light: I could see at once the route that I had cleared on my way through the forest, the sparkling river in the distance, the petrified trees. Dazzled by the sudden shock of brightness, I clamped my hands to my eyes and fell to the ground. Leaves fluttered and crackled; branches plummeted down with thunderous crashing – and then there was silence. A gust of wind whistled through the sighing treetops; another branch cracked and swung, creaking on its sinewy hinge before finally giving up the struggle and dropping with a dull thud to the earth.

That was how I discovered the grave. I had fallen by the edge of a deep crater, and through the darkness I could make out the forms of a hundred little bodies. I began digging through them, knowing that Gert was somewhere below, suffocating beneath the weight of so many lost souls. When I reached the bottom of the pit, there was nothing: only an empty jockey box. As I turned to throw it up over the edge of the pit, I felt a weight on my arm and looked down to see that it was Sipho's hand. He, too, was dead: his head lolling to one side, legs splayed, bare feet poking up in the air like tree stumps. "Is it true, *kleinnooi?*" I heard him ask, although his mouth did not move. "Are you one of them?"

And then the dream shifted. I was in our house again, although now it was empty. I ran through the rooms, calling for Pa, but there was no answer. As I opened the front door to look outside, I was stopped in my tracks by a wall of sand. I slammed the door shut, but suddenly sand was everywhere: pouring through the windows, seeping through the joints in the floor, falling in heavy sheets against the sides of the house so that the walls shook. I saw that I would be buried alive, and I screamed.

I hit my head on the underside of the raised barracks floor as I lurched into consciousness. My father's coat lay in a pile in the dirt about my feet. The empty grain sack that the khaki soldier had given me to lie on was coarse and too thin on the hard ground. I vaguely remembered him struggling to find the Dutch words to tell Ma that if she wouldn't let me stay in our own tent, there wouldn't be any space for me elsewhere.

Outside, no one stirred. A row of tents faced me, blind and silent. I wondered who lay inside them, how many had heard of my shameful banishment. They were unlikely to help me now.

Footsteps thudded overhead, and I scrambled onto my stomach, dragging myself out from beneath the veranda. The khaki who had taken me from Ma was standing on the steps, yawning, a white spot of shaving cream lingering innocently beneath one ear. When he saw me stand up, he pursed his lips and nodded as if agreeing with something neither of us had said.

"Corporal Byrne," I whispered. The words came from nowhere. And then, uncertainly, for I had never spoken his name before, I said again, "Corporal Malachi Byrne."

The soldier stopped nodding and squinted at me. He

had an alert, narrow face and a restless manner.

"What did you say?"

"Corporal Malachi Byrne." I remembered the badge that he had shown us, the picture of the leaf. "Corporal Byrne . . ."

Another soldier appeared on the step behind him, and the first one cocked his head at him. "The kid's delirious," he said.

"Corporal Byrne," I repeated, wondering what he'd just said. The words made me feel braver each time I said them.

"Who's that?" asked the second soldier.

"Your guess is as good as mine."

The second soldier tiptoed down the steps, never taking his eyes off me – as if I was an animal that might be frightened away.

"*Wie is Corporal Byrne?*" he asked in my language.

"*My vriend.*"

The soldiers looked at each other. "She says he's her friend."

"I gathered that, Parsons."

"*Waar is hy?*" asked the soldier called Parsons. I shrugged. Gert and I had last seen Corporal Byrne by the river, before we were reunited with the *laager*.

"Standerton," I said at last.

"Standerton's miles away," said Parsons.

"Look into it," said the other before tweaking his top shirt button and marching off.

I knew that the khakis reserved special treatment for

prisoners who were willing to reveal the location of rogue commandos. I didn't have any secret to share – they had already discovered our stores at Tant Minna's farm, and the *laager* had long since lost contact with any commando – but I clung to the hope that Corporal Byrne's name might just buy me continued protection.

I started wandering the rows of tents. It soon became clear from the looks I was sent that I was going to need all the help I could get. I didn't dare go back to our tent to retrieve my ration book from Ma, and it seemed unlikely that any of the women who had given me food in the past would be inclined to do so now. The children Gert and I had played with just two weeks earlier now regarded me with squint-eyed suspicion, and I wondered if they thought I might be contagious. As I walked, I became aware of a sharp, sour smell, which seemed to follow me wherever I went. I felt myself flush with shame when I realized that the smell came from my own filthy pinafore, which hadn't been washed in weeks.

A group of boys snickered loudly when they saw me approach. They had been sharing a squashed tobacco roll, sucking the smoke loudly through their teeth, shielding it from the wind with grimy palms, and they grinned at me with blackened, bleeding gums.

"How's it, Corlie?" one of them sneered.

"Leave me alone."

The next group I encountered was a gaggle of younger children. When they saw me draw near, the girls began to giggle, pussyfooting restlessly with the thrill of mischief. One of them – who was twice my height and as skinny as a reed, with a face like lemons and a bonnet too large for her head – reached out and pinched my arm as I passed by.

"Corlie Roux's a traitor," she taunted. "She's not a Boer at all."

"Get her!" shouted another, and at once the group began launching stones at me. The first few missed by a mile, but as they came closer one caught my hand. I was so stunned that at first I didn't think to run away.

"It isn't true –" I began.

Another stone hit my shoulder, and I broke into a run. The pack of children chased me halfway across the camp before their mothers started to call them back; it was too early in the day to spend so much energy buzzing about like a swarm of tsetse flies.

I stopped when I reached an upturned bull cart abandoned at the farthest corner of the camp. It was the kind of cart I'd seen the Tommies use to transport the dead at the end of each day. I ducked beneath it and pulled my knees up to my chin. I wanted to cry then, more than I ever had before in my life – but my eyes were as dry as the veld stretching beyond the prison fence. I rubbed my temples with both hands, confused by the competing desires to weep and to scream. In the end, I must have made some kind of noise, because before long a withered face poked into view.

"What's wrong, little girl?"

It was Errol Joubert, the old man who went door

to door trying to sell useless pieces of rubbish. I remembered Annie Steenkamp saying that he would try to sell someone the darkness of Egypt if he thought he could get a fair price for it. Years of smoking a tobacco pipe had turned his gray hair slightly yellow at the front. His cuticles were yellow, too, and his fingernails were as dull and cracked as old ivory keys on a piano. But the whites of his eyes were as clear and cold as frost.

"Nothing," I mumbled. Before, the space under the upturned wagon had felt almost luxurious; now his stale breath filled the air, and I stretched out my legs to create some distance between us.

"Doesn't look like nothing to me," he grinned. Most of his teeth were missing.

"You know as well as everyone else," I snapped. "My ma hates me."

"Is that so?" The old man clicked his tongue. "That's a shame, that is. A crying shame. You know what Jesus said, don't you?"

I stared at him, wishing that he would leave me alone.

"'A house divided against itself falleth,'" rasped Errol Joubert. "You know what that means?"

"I don't care!"

A white hand shot out at me as fast as a python's tongue. The next thing I knew, he had me by one arm, yellow nails digging into my skin like talons.

"That isn't the way to speak to an elder," he hissed. "You're a *hensopper!* A traitor —"

"Who told you that?"

I clamped my mouth shut and tried to pull myself from his grasp. But the old man was surprisingly strong.

"I came to help you," he said. I could tell that he was trying to smother my fear with gentle words. "Let me help you."

"Leave me alone!"

"You can sit on my knee. Make an old man happy –"

"If you don't let go of me, I'll scream!"

Stirred to fury, the old man clawed at me with his free hand through the spokes of the wagon wheel.

"And who do you think will come to rescue you?" he wheezed, battling to hold on to me as I squirmed to the farthest corner of the shelter. "Little whore!"

I glimpsed his withered arm, the one that was holding me. It was bluish-white and flecked with liver spots, sprouting a jungle of wiry gray hairs. One large vein bulged from his elbow to his hand, where it branched into three or four lumpy blue tributaries. Swallowing my fear, I lunged for the fleshy part of his forearm, sinking my teeth in as far as they would go.

Errol Joubert screamed, the exact sound a chicken makes just as its neck is being wrung. As he writhed about on the ground, clutching his arm to his chest and howling with rage, I slipped out on the other side of the wagon and scrambled to my feet.

"Come back here!" the old man cried. And then, in a nasty, desperate plea, "Little girl, come sit with me and Oom Errol will tell you a pretty tale . . ."

But I had already fled.

The copper taste of blood stayed in my mouth for the rest of that day, reminding me of my shame. I wandered the camp in a daze, following passage after passage between rows of identical tents. There had been a time when I would have quickly become lost, but weeks spent traipsing back and forth with Gert had imprinted the layout of the camp on my memory. Although I didn't make a conscious effort to avoid the block of tents that had once been home, I managed to keep to the periphery and so avoided encountering any of our immediate neighbors. Some of the faces I saw were new to me – children whose hair had not yet been shorn, women who still thought it would make a difference to complain about the lack of soap and water, who had yet to learn the futility of their rage – while the ones I recognized swam past me like ghosts, silently judging the girl who had been banished by her own mother.

As I walked, I felt something change inside me. It was as if Corlie Roux were shrinking, pressed in on all sides so that she had no choice but to grow smaller and smaller, shrinking into a tiny ball that was becoming buried in the deepest chambers of her body until – *pop!* – she hardly existed at all. Just below my skin, I could feel a protective layer begin to spread up and down my arms and legs, around my body, up and over my head. It was as hard as a calabash shell, and Corlie Roux was just a miniscule, sour seed nestled deep inside its armor. The Africans cooked calabash seeds in sugar and ate them as sweets, but not even wild animals would bother trying to eat them raw.

I am nothing, I thought. *No one loves me, and those that did are dead. So be it: I will love no one.*

I repeated this mantra to myself over and over – *I am nothing . . . I am nothing . . .* – until a voice shook me from my trance.

"Corlie Roux!"

I looked up, and there before me was Tant Minna. She grabbed me by both arms and hustled me into the nearest tent. It didn't occur to me to protest.

The tent was empty; it didn't look as if anyone had lived in there for a long time. Black flies swarmed around a forlorn campaign table that must have been left when the last of the occupants died. It seemed strange that none of the neighbors had thought to claim it.

"Say something, Corlie." Tant Minna was crouching in front of me, staring at my face with worried eyes. She wrung her hands slowly, stretching the thin, white skin over square knuckles.

"*I am nothing.*"

"What?" Her dense eyebrows – caterpillars, Gert used to call them – formed a peak beneath five deep lines that ran across her forehead. I counted them, too afraid to meet her gaze. "You're delirious, girl! When was the last time you had some water to drink?"

"I'm not thirsty."

"Don't be ridiculous. Stay here." Tant Minna disappeared outside for several moments before reappear-
ing with a slop bucket and a ladle. "Drink what's left.
Go on, do as I say."

I drank the stale water, and wondered if it had been
used to rinse dishes or worse.

"Where are you staying?"

"Beneath the khaki barracks."

"And food? Are they feeding you?"

I shrugged. Tant Minna scowled. She didn't like me
any more than Ma did, that much I knew. But I had
always felt that she might have loved me just a little –
enough to care whether I lived or died, anyway.

"I'll leave something for you there tonight."

I nodded.

"Corlie?" For the first time, I met her eyes. "He was
a good boy, Corlie."

I felt my legs threaten to buckle.

"I know. He was my brother," I said in a low voice.
Then, when my aunt didn't reply, I ventured, "Why did
Ma say I was one of them?"

Tant Minna gazed at me with a look of wonder –
almost as if she were a little child and I was some mirac-
ulous creature of her imagination – but in an instant
her expression changed, hardened. I could see that she,
too, wore a shell beneath her skin.

"What's past is past," she said.

"Tell me." I took her by the hand. "Tell me, Tant Minna."

And then, to my surprise, she sat down and started talking.

She told me how gold had been discovered four years before I was born, at an outcrop on a large ridge thirty miles south of Pretoria – an area known as the Witwatersrand. The find attracted British interest, and a fresh crop of *uitlanders* – outsiders, we called them – poured in to seize the deposit. Some of these men were opportunists and short-term speculators who left as soon as they had made a tidy profit from the mines. But a few of the men stayed on, lured by the prospect of long-term gain. My aunt told me that one of the men had bought a house on the other side of the town where Ma was still living with her parents and younger siblings.

"His name was Gordon," said Tant Minna. "Something-Gordon. There was a good six feet on him. Slender as tall grass, and fair as a daisy. Auburn hair that looked red when the light caught it. Eyes that could bewitch a young girl – and so they did. Your ma fell madly in love."

I swallowed dryly.

"At one point, there was talk of marriage, but our pa wouldn't have it. When he found out that your ma had been seeing an *uitlander,* he fair nearly tore the house down with his bellowing. But by that point, it was too late." My aunt paused. "Your ma was already pregnant with you, Corlie."

I felt my lips move, but there was no breath to form words.

"One night, our pa went out with a gang of his men to give this Gordon fellow a talking to – although Gordon had already fled. Your ma waited to hear from him, but soon someone would find out she was pregnant. When our pa suggested that she marry Morne Roux, she agreed – to preserve her dignity. She waited and waited, and then you were born, and she waited some more. But we never heard from that man Gordon again."

"He left her," I whispered.

"And she hurt – Lord, how your mother hurt." Tant Minna bit her lip, turning the pink flesh white. "Until one day, there was a change in her. She grew strong. It was as if she had decided that she would never be hurt again."

"She grew a calabash shell –"

"What's that, my girl?"

I shook my head.

Tant Minna stood up. "There's some that will say I shouldn't have told you this," she mused. "But your ma has done all the harm already, keeping it bottled up so long."

"My pa –"

"Your pa loved you as if you were his own," said Tant Minna with new firmness. "In every way, you were his child. He loved you." *He loved you even when your ma couldn't,* she seemed to say.

I nodded, and turned to leave the tent. The air inside had become stifling, and I was growing dizzy.

"Corlie –" Tant Minna pressed something into my hand: Gert's arrowhead. I didn't want to look at it, so I shoved it deep into my pocket. "It must have fallen off when they took him," my aunt explained. "I didn't tell your ma. She was so upset she didn't even notice, kept going on about what he'd said – she couldn't make any sense of it . . ."

I stopped and looked at her, almost too frightened to speak. "What did he say?" I asked.

My aunt considered me with a sad, quizzical look. "She told me he wanted to know about some lad who lived by the sea," she replied. "'What happened to the fisherman's son?' he asked. Yes, that's right. Silly, I know – but your mother insists those were his last words."

I swallowed, running my fingernail along the edge of the arrowhead in my pocket. I needed to go – now. I lifted the edge of the tent flap and left my aunt without a word.

"Stay out of the sun," said Tant Minna behind me. But by then, her voice was already as distant as a blue-bottle drumming against a closed window.

THE CALABASH SHELL

When I arrived back at the barracks, the soldier called Parsons was busy polishing a pair of boots on the stoop. I noticed that his nose was crisscrossed with red lines as fine as tiny, hatched threads. His eyelashes were golden, almost white, and the skin on his lower lip was blistered and brown from the sun.

"*My naam is Corlie Roux,*" I announced.

Parsons looked up from his polishing, and when he saw me he grinned. Something about the way he curled his lip as he squinted into the light reminded me of Gert, and I felt a stone drop to the pit of my stomach.

"Good day to you, Miss Roux," Parsons said. "Got yourself into a bit of a scuffle, I see." He nodded at the blood on my pinafore: an ugly reminder of Errol Joubert's creeping hands.

I considered the plain gold ring on his finger, and

wondered if he had children of his own. The thought occurred to me that he might even know the man who Tant Minna claimed was my real father. *My vader se naam is Gordon,* I might say. Easy as that.

Parsons's eyes would grow large, and the boyish half-grin would bloom into a smile. "Gordon?" he would say. "But I know him! He's my best friend, the only honorable man in the British Army!" Perhaps Gordon would turn out to be his cousin, or an uncle, or a neighbor from home. Suddenly, I realized that every Tommy was a potential relation: the one who hauled the death cart past the columns of tents every evening, the one who whistled as he mended holes in the fence, the one who assisted the doctor in the hospital – even the doctor himself, come to think of it. I recalled the khaki soldiers who had shot the men in our *laager,* the kindly old gent who had retrieved Lindiwe and her daughters from the bush, the beady-eyed commandant who had made us turn in our weapons.

And then I knew that I would never tell Parsons my father's name: I could not risk finding out that he was the same man who had burned our farm or torn Sipho from his mother's arms.

Instead, I crawled back under the veranda, later pretending not to hear when he returned with a bowl of scraps from the officers' mess.

"Something to keep your strength up, Corlie Roux," Parsons said. And then, realizing that I was far too proud to acknowledge his charity, he whispered, "*God seën u.*"

I must have woken at some point during the night, as I remember finding a second bowl of scraps beside the one I had emptied earlier. Tant Minna had left a corner of bread in a saucer of condensed milk, the kind of treat she might leave out for a cat. Next to it was Parsons's bowl of tepid stew and a dry biscuit. I counted two pieces of meat and a vegetable that had the consistency of cabbage. It was the finest meal I had tasted in months. As soon as I had licked every last drop from the dish, I rolled over and fell back to sleep.

When I woke up in the night, my arms and legs had marbled blue in the cold; I still had only my father's coat for cover. Tugging this more closely around my shoulders, I dreamed that it was a shield, a shell that spread and spread until it had enveloped me entirely before growing thick and hard like the walls of a cell. At first the shell made me feel safe, and I nestled into its soft contours like a baby swaddled on her mother's back. But then I realized that as the gaps filled in and the shell thickened, any trace of light was being squeezed out until at last I found myself alone, in darkness.

I dreamed that I opened my eyes and stared hard through the darkness, but all I could see were blotches of blue on black. I stared and stared until my eyes hurt so much I began to cry, and then the tears stung so much that I buried my head in my arms and chewed my knuckles to stop myself from weeping. I told myself that it was only a dream, that the shell was only my father's coat, that it was dark only because I had not yet chosen to open my eyes.

I woke to English voices. That was the first thing I noticed. The second thing I noticed was that we were in darkness.

I opened my eyes, tried to turn my head. The voices were real; I was sure of it. I wasn't dreaming.

"I can't see," I said. And then, because it seemed that no one had heard me, I said it again, more loudly this time. "*Ek kan nie sien nie!*"

I felt a hand on my shoulder, but I brushed it away and began to tear at my face with both hands. They must have blindfolded me, tied a scarf around my eyes or pulled a sack over my head. But I could feel no such thing.

My heart began to pound. "*Ek kan nie sien nie!*" I shrieked, scrambling onto all fours even as several hands grasped my legs and shoulders to keep me on my back. The hands were firm, but not rough: as soon as I ceased struggling, they withdrew. Only then did I realize that I was lying on a bed, a real bed, with a proper mattress and a thin sheet. I froze, thinking that perhaps by doing so I might become invisible to my captors. It also gave me an opportunity to try to make sense of what they were saying in English, a language that sometimes sounded like mine.

"It's a vascular problem," said one. "Burst blood vessels at the backs of the eyes."

"There's a rumor going round that the brat's half-English," said another voice. "Turned out by her own mother, the wretch. Parsons says she's been living below the barracks for the last three days – that's where he found her."

"She might have hit her head," suggested the first voice. "The thing now is to keep her still. Get some water into her, will you?"

The voices were serious, but not unfriendly. The one giving the directions sounded tired, as if he carried a great weight upon his shoulders.

"Is Parsons there? Someone should explain it to her – stop her panicking."

There was a shuffling of feet and a whispered exchange; then, a familiar voice spoke in my ear.

"Corlie? *Dit is Parsons.*"

I reached out with both arms, but he gently lowered my hands to my sides. "You're unwell," he said in my language. "Some of the women heard you crying this morning – you were saying that you couldn't see. The doctor has had a look at you, and apparently there's some bleeding in your eyes. The thing now is to get some rest. I'm going to see to it that you have enough to drink, understand? But you must be a good girl, and stay quiet." I felt him press something into my hand: something square and solid, which seemed to melt in my clammy palm. "It's only army rations, but I thought you might like some. Go on, have a taste."

Chocolate. It took me several seconds to be sure that that was what I was tasting: real chocolate, slightly chalky with age, but chocolate nonetheless. The last time I had eaten chocolate, my father had still been alive. After a few moments, the sticky sweetness was too much: I swallowed the chocolate with an almighty effort, feeling fresh tears form as I turned my face away so that Parsons wouldn't think me ungrateful.

A few days later, I felt the sun on my eyelids.

The sensation of warmth soon transformed into colors – yellow and white blotches that danced across my field of vision like tiny fireballs – and slowly, painfully, through crusted eyes I began to make out the light reflecting off the steel foot of my hospital bed.

"Parsons?" I whispered.

I thought that it might be him standing there – it was a man's figure that I could see, outlined against a window. "Pa?"

The figure edged closer, and I realized that he was leaning on crutches, with one leg tucked up in bandages. By the time he got to my bedside, I recognized the sweep of black hair, the neat mustache, and the leaf-shaped badge.

"Corlie?" he said. There was uncertainty in his voice, and – I don't think I imagined this – fear. "Is that you, Corlie Roux?"

I rubbed my eyes. "*Wie's daar?*" I asked.

There was a long silence.

"It's me, Corlie," he said at last.

BETHLEHEM

When at last I saw myself in the greasy reflection of a washstand mirror, it became clear why Corporal Byrne had not recognized me immediately. Where once my hair had grown in mousy curls was now only a thin layer of fuzz, sprouting like gray moss on my shaven head. My eyes were ringed with dark circles, and my lips were white. Watching the other children in the camp disappear into gaunt shadows of their former selves, I had not realized that I, too, had faded. My throat was always dry now, and my voice rasped; the words I mouthed rattled about in my head, making my ears pound and my eyes burn. My legs were covered in lice bites, and my arms were still bruised by Ma's hard fingers.

Corporal Byrne, on the other hand, looked much as I remembered him – taller, somehow, and bronzed by many months under an African sun. But there was sadness in his eyes.

Parsons explained that Corporal Byrne had been granted leave on account of his leg – a wound that he had sustained in battle at Elandsfontein. He had heard about the captured *laager* and our transportation to the Free State, but he'd had to wait to join a column on its way to Bloemfontein before he could reach Kroonstad.

"He says he has something to show you," said Parsons, as Corporal Byrne watched on from the bedside. "A surprise. But it will have to wait until later, when the doctor has left and the nurses are at supper."

"*'n Verrassing?*" I asked.

"That's right. But you mustn't mention it to anyone else, understand? Hospital regulations, you know."

It must have been a few hours before he returned, and I had just begun to doze off to the sound of sleeping noises from other patients in nearby beds. Corporal Byrne arrived cradling a squirming lump bundled in an army blanket.

"Corlie? Look, Corlie – look who's come to see you . . ."

He unfurled the blanket far enough to reveal a small black face fringed with white hair. Two large brown eyes peered out at me. As Corporal Byrne loosened the blanket, a long, black-tipped tail extended and curled, and two long, thin arms stretched out to me in a silent plea. The monkey's skin was pale blue beneath mottled gray fur.

"*Apie?*" I lifted my hand to touch one gray arm, and the monkey wriggled in Corporal Byrne's embrace. It was as large as a small dog, and probably weighed as much as a sack of mealie corn.

"Easy, Moet," whispered Byrne – but when the monkey refused to desist, he loosened his grasp and lowered him gently to the bed. The vervet scrambled toward me, pinching my arms through the sheets with his little claws, and drew up so close to my face that our noses were almost touching. Then, with a bark, he leaped into the air.

"He recognizes you," said Corporal Byrne with a mystified look.

"My *apie* . . ." The vervet had climbed up onto the bedpost, where he set about examining my head for any sign of insect life.

"I found him by one of the wagons, howling at the moon," said Corporal Byrne, who talked to me as if I understood. I liked listening to him even though I could only pick out a few words. "I figured you kids must have been with the *laager,* and when I saw how tame he was – well, I guessed he must have been a child's pet." He shook his head. The sadness in his eyes was the same sadness I saw in the parched, battle-scarred land beyond the wire fence: a lonely wilderness that had long since taken root deep inside us both. "I couldn't find it in my heart to just leave the poor little fella, so I took him home with me. My troop christened him Moet." Corporal Byrne pointed at the monkey so I would understand. "Moet." He pronounced it "Mo-ay."

"Moet," I repeated. "Moet."

The vervet immediately stopped fiddling with my hair and scampered to the foot of the bed. He raised himself onto his hind legs, surveying the room filled with sleeping bodies. Then he glanced over one shoulder to Corporal Byrne, his brown eyes questioning.

"He's looking for Gert," I whispered.

"Where is Gert?" asked Corporal Byrne. Seeing that I could not reply, he gathered the wee vervet in the army blanket and brought him close to my face so that I could kiss his soft, gray head.

"I'll come back tomorrow," he said.

He came back every day for two weeks. Sometimes Parsons would join him, to translate for us. He twice returned with Moet, although Parsons was clearly uncomfortable with smuggling an animal into the hospital. In the end, he convinced us that there would be plenty of time to see the monkey when I was well enough to go outside.

When Parsons was around we would talk about life before the war, and if there was no one to translate we played tic-tac-toe. Corporal Byrne drew me pictures of Canada — majestic mountains circled by handsome birds; sparkling lakes and rivers overflowing with fish; forests lurking with bears and strange, antlered horses called moose; buffalo that looked nothing like ours, with lumpish heads and handlebar horns; cabins built out of tree trunks – and I wondered if he regretted leaving his homeland for the battlefields of Africa. Once, I asked him if Canada was as beautiful as the Transvaal in the spring. Corporal Byrne had laughed, and said that it was a darn sight colder at that time of year.

One morning, he was late. I waited and waited, eventually climbing up onto the window ledge by my bed so that I could see him when he approached.

Outside, the camp was mostly still. Everyone seemed to have retreated into their tents, and the few British soldiers that remained on Steyn Street seemed to be in a hurry to get into the barracks buildings. I looked across the ward at all the empty beds, and realized that almost all the patients had left. Those that could walk had returned to their tents, and those that remained – two frail figures at the far end by the door – were too ill to know that the hospital was empty.

I considered leaving, but then I remembered that I had nowhere to go. My clothes were folded in a pile by my bed. Unnerved by the eerie silence, and desperate to do something, I got dressed.

As I laced my boots with fumbling fingers – it was as if my hands had forgotten the familiar sequence of looping, threading, and pulling tight – the hospital door was flung open to a chorus of voices.

> *The nations not so blest as thee,*
> *Must in their turn to tyrants fall,*
> *Must in, must in, must in their turn to tyrants fall!*

I recognized the officer called Stevens, the doctor, and the gravediggers, as well as a cohort of young soldiers. They poured through the hospital, singing at the tops of their lungs.

While thou shalt flourish, shalt flourish great and free,
The dread and envy of them all!

It was a fearful racket. Their bellowing voices echoed through the empty ward as the men stomped their feet and clapped their hands, whistling and whooping with delirious joy. They didn't appear to notice me.

Rule, Britannia!
Britannia, rule the waves:
Britons never, never, never will be slaves!

And then, almost as quickly as they had appeared, they were gone. Their voices carried on outside, singing a different tune.

O Lord, our God, arise,
Scatter her enemies,
And make them fall!
Confound their politics,
Frustrate their knavish tricks,
On Thee our hopes we fix,
God save us all . . .

I listened to the voices become more distant, until at last only the wisp of a melody remained.

Then I saw him, standing in the doorway, his handsome face creased into a smile.

"It's over, Corlie," said Corporal Byrne. "The war's over."

I stood up, sensing that he had said something important. Corporal Byrne came closer, his movements taut with excitement. His voice was soft, but urgent.

"The last of the commandos surrendered yesterday at Rooiwal. There's to be a treaty at Vereeniging."

I couldn't help smiling at the way he pronounced it, garbling the guttural sounds with his crisp, clipped accent. Then I began to understand what he meant. The commandos must have run out of food, or ammunition, or perhaps both. Too many men had wives and children dying in the camps, and saw that the war was destined to be lost. They had given up.

I sat back down on the bed, my mind racing. What would this mean for the others – for Oom Sarel, and Danie and Andries? For Sipho and Lindiwe? Where would we go? Would we be punished for having the audacity to survive?

Corporal Byrne must have noticed that I didn't share his excitement, because the smile faded as he perched on the bed opposite mine.

"The republics will become a part of the Empire," he said slowly, as if by speaking clearly I would be able to understand his English. "*Die Transvaal en die Vry*

Staat." He clasped his hands together, motioning a union. "*Britse.*"

British.

"But they will be granted self-government," continued Byrne in a hopeful voice. He might as well have been talking to the walls. "They will be as good as free . . ."

I shook my head in disbelief.

Corporal Byrne stood up, and extended one hand.

"Come, Corlie," he said. "It's time to leave this place."

THE SEA OF GALILEE

We found my mother with a group of women preparing to board a cattle car for Standerton. There was little rejoicing: on every face, I could see grief for those they were leaving behind and grim uncertainty about what they would find waiting for them back home. I saw Heila Du Preez standing alone at the end of the line, and for a moment I thought of calling out to her. Then I noticed that Frikkie was nowhere to be seen, and realized that the spider bite must have been worse than we'd thought.

Each family had been provided with a tent and a month's rations. As we watched the women turn in their ration cards, I held Corporal Byrne's hand tightly.

"Don't make me go with her," I whispered.

Corporal Byrne looked down at me. Parsons must have told him of my shameful eviction; he must have explained the bruises on my arms.

"Which one is she?" he asked. "*Jou moeder?*"

I pointed. Ma still towered over the other women, head held high. Hansie stood at her side, gripping her skirts, wide blue eyes agog at the commotion. He saw me first.

"Corlie!"

Ma smacked him before she even had a chance to see me; it was as if he had uttered a forbidden word, a most grievous blasphemy. When at last she picked me out, hovering on the fringes of the group, next to the Canadian soldier, her eyes narrowed.

"I didn't die, Ma," I said, just loud enough for her to hear. "They wouldn't let me die."

Of course, in my heart of hearts I wanted my mother to love me. But I also knew that she would never forgive me for who I was – any more than I could forgive her for betraying Sipho and Lindiwe. We were at a stalemate, just like in the war.

My mother glanced around at the other women, as if to see if I had shamed her before the group. But no one was paying any attention.

"They look after their own," said Ma. "They deserve you, Corlie Roux."

And then, taking Hansie by the arm, she turned and pushed her way deeper into the crowd.

"Well," said Corporal Byrne when at last we lost all sight of her. "I suppose that's that."

I looked up into his face, and I smiled.

We said good-bye to Parsons and joined the military cavalcade that was headed for Ladysmith. When I realized that we would be stopping at Bethlehem, I begged Corporal Byrne to take me to the African camp. We had just a few hours before our train would depart, but I needed to find out what had happened to Lindiwe and her family.

Until I saw the vestiges of the African settlement, I would not have believed that there existed a prison more deprived than ours. We were led to the camp by an elderly African known among the khakis as Old September. He remained silent as Corporal Byrne and I took in the desolate scene. Apart from some barbed wire and a few ramshackle buildings constructed of corrugated iron, there was nothing to see. Old September pointed out the abandoned packing crates, grain bags, and tarpaulins that the inmates had used to improvise shelter; he led us through the dry fields where they had been forced to grow their own food against the odds of a cruel winter and barren soil.

I asked our guide if he had known a woman called Lindiwe, but Old September only shook his head.

"She had two little girls," I explained in Dutch. "And a son called Sipho. He was taken to a POW camp, I don't know where. They were going to lay charges . . ."

The old man's cloudy eyes seemed to fill with light.

"Sipho?" he said. "The lad who killed a fat Boer?"

I felt my heart leap inside me. "Where is he?" I begged. "Do you know?"

The light in Old September's eyes began to fade, as if dampened by my excitement.

"We heard of him from some Sotho fighters who were serving with the British. The whole camp heard. The boy was executed with a group of white men. He had a white man's hanging, an honorable death."

I froze: it must be a mistake.

"There was a trial," continued Old September. "He wouldn't apologize for what he did. He said that the only white man who ever treated him right was dead, and that his only white friend was locked up in a khaki concentration camp." The old man considered me. "That was you, was it?"

I nodded, unable to speak.

Old September grunted. "Well, he said you'd understand." The old man smiled a toothless smile, gazing over the tops of the thorn trees. "That's what I heard, anyhow."

Walking back to the station, Corporal Byrne asked me to hold Moet. He had devised a sling for the monkey, who could not keep up with us on foot over the rocky terrain – even though Corporal Byrne still had to walk slowly because of his leg. I knew that Corporal Byrne thought it would comfort me, to hold the orphaned vervet close to my chest and nuzzle the soft fur on the back of his head.

As Moet grumbled in the sling, I pressed my face next to his and wept.

I never did find out what happened to Lindiwe and her daughters. Like so many others, their names were lost to history.

It was only later that I found out that the English queen had died. Newspapers were so scarce that many of the Tommies themselves hadn't known until months after the fact. There was a new king on the throne, I was told: King Edward. Now, he was my king, too.

That was when I began to appreciate the toll that the war had taken on the Tommies, when I realized that the sadness in Corporal Byrne's eyes – the same sadness that I read in the faces of the other men – sprung from a loss of something that they had once believed to be noble and true. As I listened to them speak, I heard admiration in their voices for their foe, the Boer guerrilla fighters. And admiration for the women in the camps, too.

"You can't blame 'em for giving it their best shot. If someone tried to boot me off my farm, I'd fight 'im tooth and nail," said one young khaki over a dinner of tinned beef and flour biscuits. The others had murmured their agreement, nodding sheepishly as they pretended not to look at me – the half-English, half-Boer girl in their midst.

There were thirty or so men in the column – combatants, mostly, freshly returned from battles at Tweebosch and Onverwacht. One arrived having just had a foot amputated; within the week, the doctor traveling with us was compelled to amputate the same leg up to the knee, and we had all listened to his muffled cries from inside a hastily constructed medical tent. Another, a bugle boy just fourteen years old, died of his shrapnel wounds that same night.

It's no wonder that the others did not have the energy to be rowdy or raucous during the celebrations that followed the war's end. Enough of them had seen the horrors of the camps that no one seemed to begrudge my presence. Perhaps I reminded some of them of the little daughters they had left at home. I liked to think that we wouldn't be so very different.

In the evenings, splints and dressings would be refreshed around the campfire, cigars would be lit, and English songs sung. The one that was always the most popular was "Good-bye, Dolly Gray":

I have come to say good-bye, Dolly Gray,
It's no use to ask me why, Dolly Gray,
There's a murmur in the air, you can hear it everywhere,
It's the time to do and dare, Dolly Gray . . .

The one who led the singing was a rosy-cheeked soldier called Broadwater. Most of the time, he was an object of fun for the rest of the troop – his pink ears

stuck out like a baby elephant's, and he was so skinny his
uniform hung off him like a scarecrow's rags – but in the
evenings, he was the star entertainer. Young Broadwater
had a voice like a bugle horn, warm and warbling, and as
he knelt on one knee before me he would throw out both
arms in a ridiculous display of mock emotion, making
me blush and the other men hoot and clap with delight.

> *Good-bye, Dolly, I must leave you, though it breaks my heart*
>   *to go,*
> *Something tells me I am needed at the front to fight the foe . . .*

As the song built to its climax, Moet would leap in
circles around us, mimicking the serenade with squeaks
and howls of excitement.

> *See, the boys in blue are marching and I can no longer stay,*
> *Hark! I hear the bugle calling – good-bye, Dolly Gray!*

Something strange was happening to me. Much as I
continued to hate what the British had done to my
family, I found that I could no longer hate the soldiers
themselves. There had been a time when I would fill
with pride listening to the women boast of their husbands' bravery on commando. Now, things were no
longer quite as clear-cut. It wasn't just that my father
had been one of them. From the Great Karoo to the
East Transvaal, and from the mighty Limpopo to the
Cape of Good Hope, generations had tried to claim a

part of Africa. My country had been watered by the blood of men from all corners of the globe – English and Dutch, Canadian and Irish, African and Indian.

Could I forgive them, these weary fighters, these faces around the fire? Old men, young men, who had done as their leaders bade them? The ones who killed Sipho, who watched as my little brother faded from this life, who robbed my mother of her last ounce of dignity? Could Lindiwe and her daughters – if indeed they were still alive – ever forgive us? I knew that the answer to these questions depended on the future, not the past. We would create a new country while the old one would dissolve into myth.

One of Corporal Byrne's comrades explained to me that many of the captured commandos had been exiled to the farthest reaches of the British Empire: to the Caribbean, to Ceylon. He said that they would only be allowed to come back to Africa if they swore an oath of allegiance to the British king.

Andries and Danie, and Oom Sarel if he had survived, would surely be among those who were exiled. I tried to imagine them on board a heaving vessel, peering through the foggy spray of the sea, waiting to sight land a thousand miles away. I wondered if they had been sad to watch their home disappear, but then I reminded myself that it's impossible to feel homesick for a place that no longer exists.

From Corporal Byrne's drawings of Canada and from what he told me of his people, who lived in places called Lacombe and Medicine Hat, I knew that home now lay somewhere else. This thought was exciting, but it also filled me with a strange loneliness. So, as I cuddled Moet in his sling at night, I told him the story I had once told Gert, of the fisherman's son who discovered a monster washed up on the shore.

"The boy had gone on a grand adventure," I told the purring vervet. "He had set sail for faraway lands, to find the monster's mythical lair.

"One night, a storm had torn his ship to shreds, and the boy woke up alone on a strange island. The fisherman's son didn't know that it took both courage and wisdom to be scared, or that he had proved himself brave and wise during the long night," I said.

"He could have done any one of a number of things. He could have shouted out to a distant goatherd, begged for help. He could have buried his head in his arms and wept. He could have walked straight into the sea, and so sealed the watery fate that he had only just escaped. Instead, he stood up – slowly, for his limbs ached and his head threatened to explode at the slightest movement – and began to walk toward the horizon."

We traveled in convoy by army wagon across the scorched countryside. Out on the veld, the land smelled of men: of salt and earth and musty leather. Every farm we passed told a tale of brutal eviction and destruction. Animal carcasses bleached by the sun sat sentry along the rutted tracks where once farmers had led their cattle to pasture. Odd bits of furniture – pieces of a rocking chair, an abandoned dowry chest, a bundle of kitchen utensils, a child's wax doll whose arms and legs had started to melt in the heat – lay scattered across the parched plain at the spots where their owners had abandoned all but the most necessary luggage. Roofless whitewashed houses, now no more than shells, haunted the empty landscape. Many were licked black where the flames had risen around their walls.

I wished that we could have paid one final visit to the farm that had once been my home – not to see what had become of it, but to place one last stone atop Pa's grave. I might even have placed one there for my real father, whoever – wherever – he was. But the column was not going anywhere near Amersfoort, and we did not have enough time to make the detour ourselves. I told myself that it made no difference. When I learned to speak English well enough, I would weave Pa into the stories I planned to tell Corporal Byrne; in that way, Pa would always be with me.

Corporal Byrne and I parted ways with the troop at Pietermaritzburg and walked the rest of the way to La Lucia. I had always dreamed of seeing the sea – of standing on the spot where land meets water, where the world as we know it becomes strange and beautiful and new again. And when I heard the first seabird's cry, I had to swallow the tears that seemed to rise from somewhere deep inside me, dissolving once and for all my calabash armor. The ancient cave dwellers who had lived on this coast long before my people came – had they felt this same sense of wonder when first they sighted foreign ships on the horizon? When we arrived at the bluffs, I was surprised to see that the ocean stretching out before us was not blue, but a frothing gray-green color. The bouldered beach below was strewed with seaweed, broken mussel shells, and shimmering purple stones worn smooth by the tide.

"*Dit is die See van Galilëe,*" I told Corporal Byrne. It was even more beautiful than I had imagined.

Together, we walked to the water's edge.

EPILOGUE

The culmination of a decades-long Scramble for Africa, the Anglo-Boer War (October 1899 – May 1902) was fought between the British Empire and the two independent Boer republics: the South African Republic (Transvaal) and the Orange Free State. It was the longest and bloodiest British war fought between 1815 and 1914. Firsthand witnesses included a number of prominent figures of the day and later decades – among them Winston Churchill, Mohandas Gandhi, Robert Baden-Powell, Rudyard Kipling, and Arthur Conan Doyle.

Roughly 8,600 Canadians volunteered to fight in the war, making this the first time that large contingents of Canadian troops served abroad. Claiming 22,000 British lives, as well as the lives of between 6,000 and 7,000 Boer fighters, the conflict came to represent the end of an era of "great" imperial wars. More than 26,000 Boer women and children perished in the British camps. The number of African casualties remains unknown, but is estimated at over 20,000.

Soon after the signing of the Treaty of Vereeniging, Britain granted limited autonomy to the occupied regions – a concession that would eventually lead to the establishment of the Union of South Africa in 1910.